THE FORTUNES OF TEXAS

Follow the lives and loves of a complex family with a rich history and deep ties in the Lone Star State

FORTUNE'S FAMILY SECRETS

With Archibald Fortune's death comes the revelation of a stunning secret: The Emerald Ridge scion had three separate families and one child he'd always longed to find! Can his shocked children come together to find Archibald's missing heir and claim the family inheritance—or will strife tear them apart?

WEDDED TO A FORTUNE

Gia Leonetti is about to score the contract of her lifetime—if only she can convince Penn Fortune that her family's wines are a perfect fit for his hotels. The last thing she expects is for their Vegas meeting to result not only in a slam dunk business partnership...but also a spur-of-the-moment marriage! What happens in Vegas, stays in Vegas. Or does it?

Dear Reader,

The Fortunes of Texas books are always such fun books to write, and I'm honored once again to be part of this world with my second Fortunes of Texas book. This time two wealthy people who haven't been lucky in love are going to challenge the long-held belief of "what happens in Vegas, stays in Vegas." Not this time!

When Penn and Gia wake up married in Las Vegas, even the fact they both have oodles of money can't stop the post office. Nope, their signed marriage certificate is in the mail before they can catch it. Plan B is to get an annulment when they return to Emerald Ridge, Texas. But between a smoldering attraction and landing in an empty field during a raging storm, Penn decides marriage to Gia is not the worst thing to ever happen to him. They are pretty much made for each other.

Now he has to convince her that a practical marriage, a "true partnership," is the only way to go. Love? Not required. Unfortunately, Gia disagrees. Love is most definitely required. What happens next is a whole lot of fun as we watch both of them fall in love without planning to do anything of the sort. The best kind of love is one that hits you when you least expect it.

Heatherly

WEDDED TO A FORTUNE

HEATHERLY BELL

Special thanks and acknowledgment are given to Heatherly Bell for her contribution to The Fortunes of Texas: Fortune's Family Secrets miniseries.

Recycling programs for this product may not exist in your area.

ISBN-13: 978-1-335-14335-8

Wedded to a Fortune

For questions and comments about the quality of this book, please contact us at CustomerService@Harlequin.com.

Harlequin Enterprises ULC
22 Adelaide St. West, 41st Floor
Toronto, Ontario M5H 4E3, Canada
www.Harlequin.com

HarperCollins Publishers
Macken House, 39/40 Mayor Street Upper,
Dublin 1, D01 C9W8, Ireland
www.HarperCollins.com

Printed in Lithuania

Bestselling author **Heatherly Bell** was born in Tuscaloosa, Alabama, but lost her accent by the time she was two. After leaving Alabama, Heatherly lived with her family in Puerto Rico and Maryland before being transplanted kicking and screaming to the California Bay Area. She now loves it here, she swears. Except the traffic.

Books by Heatherly Bell

The Fortunes of Texas: Fortune's Family Secrets

Wedded to a Fortune

Montana Mavericks: The Trail to Tenacity

The Maverick's Christmas Countdown

Harlequin Special Edition

Charming, Texas

Winning Mr. Charming
The Charming Checklist
A Charming Christmas Arrangement
A Charming Single Dad
A Charming Doorstep Baby
Once Upon a Charming Bookshop
Her Fake Boyfriend
The Ex Next Door
Overboard for the Holidays

The Fortunes of Texas: Hitting the Jackpot

Winning Her Fortune

Visit the Author Profile page
at Harlequin.com for more titles.

Dedicated to Laurel Whitney,
a loyal reader from Salem, New Hampshire

Chapter One

Gia Leonetti adjusted her cell phone so her face could be clearly seen by her brother Leo and sister Antonia.

"Can you see my happy smile all the way from here in Las Vegas?" Gia grinned into the phone from the back seat of the limousine.

"Good news I take it?" Leo asked.

"We don't call her Glamorous Gorgeous Gia for nothing," her sister Antonia said. "Triple G is the family closer."

Her siblings were both still at the corporate offices of Leonetti Vineyards in Emerald Ridge, Texas, given the fluorescent lighting and dark wood furnishings in the background. By Gia's calculations, due to the time difference, both Leo and Antonia should be headed home to their spouses but they both worked long hours as the CEO and CFO of their family business.

Gia snapped her fingers. "I just got four hotelier accounts for partnerships with Leonetti Vineyards today alone. I've been busy."

"Whoa," Leo said. "Our ancestors would be proud. It's almost like you know what you're doing."

All three of them laughed at the truth of this. After years floundering and trying to find her place in the family business, Gia had arrived. She'd always been a team player and outgoing by nature, so head of marketing wound up a perfect fit for her sunny nature.

She'd been shocked and embarrassed to learn Leonetti wines were not being carried in any of the Fortune Resorts hotels. They only served the best European wines, apparently. If nothing else, she would convince Penn Fortune that the Leonetti brand could easily compete with what they carried. Her family's vineyard had been modeled after the original one in Tuscany and had the same recipes.

"Wish me all the luck because my toughest meeting is next," Gia admitted. "I'm on my way to the swankiest hotel on the strip, the Fortune Resort Hotel."

Antonia gaped. "We've been trying to get in for years with no luck. Even our family Fortune connections didn't help."

"What can I say? I'm talented and persistent. From what I understand, my meeting is with Penn Fortune himself."

"How did you manage that? He's notoriously difficult to pin down," Leo said.

"I let it drop that I'm also from Emerald Ridge, so maybe that helped."

Penn had recently moved from Houston to Emerald Ridge, and though she hadn't ever had the pleasure of an introduction, his reputation went far and wide. He was incredibly wealthy, part of a rather interesting branch of the Fortune family. Since both Leo and Antonia were married to Fortunes from another branch, Gia had heard plenty. Unfortunately, rumors were swirling around Emerald Ridge regarding their rather sketchy family past.

Gia didn't judge, because *everyone* had issues, though Penn's family seemed to have more drama than most. His father, Archibald Fortune, had three different families with three different wives, and none of them had known about each other. For *decades*. How he'd managed to pull that off

Gia would never know, but she guessed someone with all his money would have plenty of resources at his disposal.

She couldn't imagine it—being so close to her own family that she liked to believe she'd know if there was anything even remotely scandalous going on. Either way, she didn't concern herself with small-town gossip. Gia loved people, which made it easy to make friends. She'd simply make friends with Penn and never once mention his odd family dynamics. People were, after all, far more than their family drama.

"I'm here, so I'll get off the phone now and do my thing." Gia shimmied her shoulders. "I'll fly home tomorrow."

"Good luck!"

Gia waved to her siblings and stowed her phone in her purse. She glanced out the window at the palm trees that lined the massive driveway of the Fortune Resort Hotel, across from the equally luxurious Venetian. The driver pulled into the porte cochere, filled with Rolls-Royces and Lamborghinis, then drove smoothly onto the red-carpeted entrance. The door opened and Gia stepped out, pausing for several long moments to take in the place's grandeur. The Fortune Resort Hotel was the most opulent on the strip.

The facade was a fusion of gold-tinted glass and sleek marble. A grand fountain at the entrance burst streams of water in a choreography of colored lights and music. Inside, the marble parquet floors shimmered as she walked toward the elevators along white Roman columns with gold accents. The cathedral ceilings were painted with art worthy of a museum. Farther back, she heard the din of the slot machines and caught a glimpse of the high rollers playing roulette.

Gia entered the elevator, punched in the privacy code she'd been given after her appointment confirmation, and began her ascent to the penthouse floor.

A hint of the smell of expensive cigars greeted her, and

floral arrangements of fresh orchids and jasmine on either side of the elevator added a subtle and unmistakable fragrance. Gratified to find her presentation of wines for the flights she'd assembled had arrived on time, she introduced herself to the secretary.

"Mr. Fortune is ready for you. He said to take you inside the moment you arrived," the woman said, pushing the cart with the wine bottles toward the ornate door.

Gia followed her inside. The secretary smiled and quickly left the room, shutting the doors behind her.

Gia felt like she'd entered the lion's den, and so far the lion didn't seem to notice she'd arrived. Maybe he wanted to paw at his toy a bit before he devoured her for a little snack. *Okay, Gia. Calm down. No need to be nervous. This is your wheelhouse.* Still, she couldn't help but be intimidated by this man, who stared at a piece of paper on his desk as if it had sucked all the joy out of him. She would hate to be in the position of the person who'd written him that letter. It seemed like any moment he'd growl.

She'd only seen photos of Penn Fortune in periodicals such as *Forbes* but that had never prepared her to see him up close and personal. His golden good looks made him almost intimidating.

Instead of waiting until he deigned to notice her, Gia put her bag down and went about setting up the flights. Once someone tasted their wines, they had a difficult time saying no to her. She removed her carefully packaged wine goblets and bottles and went at the first bottle with her silver corkscrew. This light and cherry-infused merlot was her best ice breaker. Her previous appointment had ordered seven cases.

"Here, let me help." Penn appeared at her side, taking the corkscrew from her.

"Oh," she said, losing her train of thought when he touched her hand. "I didn't see you there."

Her entire body buzzed with awareness. For the love of good wine, this man was *gorgeous*. As a brunette, she'd always been a sucker for blonds. Ones who wore Armani suits and walked like sleek jaguars were among her favorites. To top it all off, Penn had beard stubble that made her want to rub against him like a cat. His green eyes were deep and dark. *Oh, good grief, get a hold of your damn self!* She didn't want word about any unprofessional exchange with Penn getting back to her family.

"Um, that's okay. I've done this four times today, and I don't mind."

"No one offered to help you?" He slid her a panty-melting grin that turned her insides to mush.

"I—I don't need help."

"Maybe so, but I'll gladly be your assistant." He easily slipped off the cork and then went to the next bottle. "I assume you want it to breathe."

She nodded.

"I'm sorry if I was rude when you first came in," Penn said, opening the next one—an almond-infused cabernet sauvignon her sister Bella, their vintner, raved about. It had won a blue ribbon last year. "Believe me, I didn't mean to ignore you."

"That's fine, I assumed you were wrapping up something important."

"It's been a rough day, yeah." He set the bottle down, then went to the next one. "But no reason to keep a beautiful woman waiting. I promise not to do it again."

She sucked in a breath at those words because he'd said them with a hint of flirtation and a sideways grin.

While he opened the remaining bottles, Gia went about pouring the first flight.

"I… I want to thank you for this meeting. My family has tried to get into Fortune Resort before without any luck."

"Apparently we both now live in Emerald Ridge," he said. "I can't turn away a neighbor. But the truth is, we only carry selections of high-priced European wines, which our customers much prefer. South of France and Italy. That's probably why no one ever wanted to waste your time with a meeting."

"Leonetti Vineyards has been around for over a century. I think if you give our vintages a chance, we won't disappoint," she murmured, tossing her hair back.

Yes, she was starting to flirt a little bit, too. Why not? She was single, he was single.

"Yeah?"

"Absolutely. Every hotelier I met with today bought a case of our wines, even multiple ones. The wine sells itself." She offered him a goblet with the first taste.

He took a sip of the wine and cocked his head. "That *is* good."

She smiled at him again, mentally preparing to go into her presentation. As Antonia once said, Gia could talk to a statue and get it to respond. Penn was far from a statue even if he did have a likeness to a Greek god.

"I have to confess, your hotel is the most luxurious one I've visited today."

"That's my evil plan. Luxury attracts high-end customers. They can never seem to get enough." His eyes drank her in and she did not miss the slow, deliberate slide up her body.

Thankfully, today she wore her sleek red dress with a modest hemline that fit like a glove. They were *officially* flirting. She didn't want a relationship after her last disaster but something temporary might be exactly what she needed right now.

If she ventured a guess, it might be exactly what he wanted, too. Besides, she'd never have to worry this man was after her family money. He had plenty of his own.

Hmm. What was that saying about what happens in Vegas stays in Vegas?

"Aren't you going to have some?" Penn asked, offering her a goblet. "I hate to drink alone."

No one else had asked her to join them before, but with Penn as the last stop it should be fine.

"I usually don't, but why not?" She accepted the glass and brought it to her lips. "I don't have anywhere else to be until I catch my plane tomorrow morning."

"I'm honored." He carried his goblet over to the leather couch in his office and took a seat. "Tell me about yourself, Gia."

"Of course." She launched into her presentation. "Leonetti Vineyards was established in the 1900s, a family business that has attracted the support of plenty of celebrities. In fact, Jackie Kennedy Onassis loved my grandfather and often visited. I'm the head of marketing, as you know, and my brother Leo is the CEO. My sister Antonia is the CFO, and Bella is our vintner. We—"

Penn held up a broad palm. "All interesting, but I'm asking about you. Not your family, or the wine. *You.*"

Gia didn't have words. No one had asked about her specifically. She would normally turn this around on him, ask *him* the questions, but he'd stumped her by catching her off guard. Gia helped herself to another taste as she pulled her thoughts together. Damn, this cabernet went down so smoothly it was like drinking grape juice with a bite. She needed a case for herself.

"Um, well, I work a lot."

“So do I.” He cocked his head and studied her. “No one special?”

“Not at the moment. And you?”

“No one.” He stood to rejoin her, taking another taste. “I have to admit, this wine is addictive.”

She raised her goblet to his. “I can give you a good deal if you’ll give us half a chance. You won’t regret it.”

“I know I won’t.”

Another smile, and Gia knew she was in trouble here for reasons that had nothing to do with wine.

Chapter Two

From the moment Gia Leonetti walked into his office and he'd looked up from his desk, Penn Fortune decided he'd buy whatever wine she was selling. She could be selling moisturizer or women's hair products and he'd ask her where to sign.

She didn't know he'd flown in his private jet today just to take this meeting himself. While he'd never met her, he'd noticed her in Emerald Ridge from a distance, since they obviously frequented the same circles. She had a flawless beauty with espresso-brown hair and dark eyes. Her sensual mouth tempted him beyond distraction, her lips looking lusher the longer he stared. He was intensely attracted to her but couldn't involve himself in anything permanent. If this were to happen, they'd both have to agree it couldn't go far.

With his family genealogy, he'd decided not to ruin any children brought into the world with his regrettable Fortune DNA. He didn't have any faith in marriage, either, after discovering his own father had tricked three different families and left a mess after his death. No, it was far better to remain unattached with less chance of hurting each other. He hoped Gia felt the same way. Something casual could work. He'd be discreet and so would she.

Penn poured more wine into the goblets, both for her and himself. He'd ended all his business meetings and tomorrow he'd fly back to Emerald Ridge. This trip to Vegas was a welcome break from the drama and scandal. Once he returned to Texas, he'd inevitably get sucked back into the mess that had become his dysfunctional family. After a couple of months of indecision, he'd reluctantly joined the rest of his siblings in the search for their missing half brother. He'd been studying the latest update from the PI they'd hired when Gia walked into his office. Nothing new to report from the investigator. The whole thing frustrated Penn to the point he regretted his involvement in the search for his brother nearly every day.

He'd wanted nothing to do with the terms of his father's will, but if he didn't join in the search for the missing brother, no one would get their inheritance. When his brother, Hayes, and their mother begged him to get involved, he'd finally relented.

He turned to face Gia. "I'm sure you've heard about my family, given your brother and sister are married to other Fortunes."

"I've heard a few things but I don't like to indulge in petty gossip about other people's families."

Penn had to chuckle. "You might be the *only* one. Just so you know, my hotels are not connected to my father's Fortune dynasty. This is my business and it was never any part of his holdings."

Damn, when she smiled at him like that, he completely lost his train of thought. It took him a moment to recover.

"My father made his money in the airline business. I'm in the hotel business."

"I was sorry to hear about your father. My condolences."

"Yeah, thanks." He raked a hand through his hair. "We were close before he died but my feelings changed when I found out he was a liar who had married three women and had another child with a fourth. My poor mother never had a clue. Neither did I, of course."

"I'm so sorry. That's terrible." She handed him another goblet of wine.

Penn slammed it down.

Gia held up her hand. "You're not supposed to—"

"Sorry, guess I'm a little bitter." He reached for another goblet and took a sip. "I know, I should savor it. It's excellent, first-class wine, by the way."

"You really mean that?" she asked.

"Yeah—and I'm not the type to lie about it just to make you feel better."

"I wouldn't expect you to. You're a good businessman and your reputation precedes you."

"Listen, I don't have to think about this anymore. You've got a deal. We'll carry your wines here at Fortune Resort Hotel. Immediately." He offered his hand. "Shake on it for now? I can have contracts drawn up tomorrow."

Her smile was like the sun. "Thank you. You won't regret it. I'll give you my personal cell phone and please feel free to call me anytime you have any questions."

"Fine, fine. Why don't we close the deal in Emerald Ridge once we're both home." Now that he was done tasting, Penn filled a goblet and offered one to Gia. "To our new partnership."

The stress he'd been under for weeks suddenly dissipated… and it wasn't because of the wine. It was because of Gia, so beautiful and kind. He didn't open up to many people, but he felt comfortable talking to her about the mess his life had become.

"The funny thing is, I always wanted a family of my own. Marriage, kids, the whole white picket fence thing. But that can't happen anymore." Penn shook his head, exhaling a long breath.

"Why not?"

"I wouldn't want to risk it. I've already seen what a disaster marriage can be. The only issue is I want children, so I'm not sure what I'm going to do about that." He chuckled. "I suppose I should adopt and make sure the poor kid has none of my DNA passed down."

"I've always wanted children, too. But lately, I'm not sure about marriage, either." She lowered her gaze. "My last relationship didn't end well. Turns out he was after my money. He broke my heart, but I guess encountering fortune hunters is par for the course with people like us."

She looked so gloomy he automatically reached for her. If she didn't want him to touch her, she'd stop him and that would be the end of it. But she didn't stop him and leaned into the slow fingertip caress he gave the curve of her jawline. They were standing very close to each other.

Penn chuckled. "Maybe we should get married just to have a partner in life. A business arrangement. It's what we both want."

Another gloomy, pensive look from Gia, but she forced a laugh. "Maybe so. But I'll never marry for anything less than true love."

Penn heard a lot of hope in those words, and before he could stop himself, he lowered his head and kissed her. Her lush lips were soft and he took the kiss deeper. She responded eagerly, gripping the lapels of his jacket. He lowered his hand to her behind and pulled her tight against him.

"Gia, I should tell you… I'm not looking for a relationship right now. But this, if you want tonight, I can do that. I know how to be discreet."

"That's all I want, too. I certainly don't want my family to find out about this. Just one night will be fine."

He kissed her again, even more passionately this time, holding her taut against him.

When he broke the kiss, Gia gazed up at him with shimmering eyes. "Do you have separate living quarters here?"

"Yes."

He took her hand and led her out the door of his executive suite and straight into the separate adjoining one.

Chapter Three

The moment Gia opened her eyes she shut them again. It was way too bright in this room. She pulled the covers over her head and realized she was naked. Not a stitch of clothing on her…oh my lord, were those her black panties thrown partially over the lampshade? Her head pounding, she almost fell out of bed the moment she realized she wasn't alone. There was the body of a man inches away from her on the same bed, sleeping on his stomach. Golden hair, taut and muscled arms, hard male angles. Penn Fortune in all his male glory.

Gia groaned. Okay, this was bad. *Very bad.* She'd obviously had sex with Penn. Memories of last night came flooding back. Yes, they were both a little inebriated on great wine, but thankfully, she could still recall the moment she'd made the decision to sleep with Penn. Gia hadn't been this attracted to a man in…ever. He hadn't talked her into a damn thing. She was in control, and in this bed on her own cognizance. She didn't regret a moment of last night.

On the other hand, she'd never done anything even remotely like this before and wondered if she should just grab her clothes and slip quietly out of here. But that didn't seem right, either. They were going to have to see each other in passing since they both lived in Emerald Ridge, especially now that they were in a business partnership together. This time what happened in Vegas wouldn't *stay* here. She remembered Penn had talked about being discreet. Good thing because if her family found out about this, they wouldn't be happy. But it was also none of their business.

Either way, her throbbing head meant she needed water. She wrapped a sheet around her body and shuffled to the carafe of water on the dresser. There was a paper near it, partially damp, so she picked it up to move it somewhere safer. Naturally curious, Gia couldn't help but take a brief perusal of the document, which appcared to be some kind of certificate.

It couldn't be, though. Penn was playing a prank on her, right?

The paper read *Official Marriage Certificate of the State of Nevada*, dated yesterday, and issued from the Lovers Lane Fortune Chapel to Penn Fortune and Gia Leonetti. She saw her signature, clear as day. At that moment, she also noticed the shiny ring on her finger and gasped.

"What? What's happening?"

Penn startled awake, threw the covers off and emerged from the bed. Yep, he was naked, too, and Gia averted her eyes before he grabbed his boxers and pulled them on.

"Is this a joke?" Gia waved the certificate. "I don't remember any of this. Where did this come from? Is it from one of those novelty shops around here?"

"What is it?" Penn reached her side and took the certificate from her, his eyes bugging out as he read. He rubbed his eyes. "I…what…did we?"

"Did we get married last night?"

They both said the words at the same time.

Penn was studying the certificate with the same intensity he'd given yesterday to that piece of paper that had clearly robbed him of joy. His finger rolled over the raised official seal.

"This can't be real, can it?" His eyes were narrowed and

staring like lasers into the paper, daring it to just *try* and contradict him.

Gia shook her head, laughed and slapped her forehead. "Of course not. I mean, who would let two people get married so quickly? This takes months of preparation. This can't be legal!"

Then they both stared at each other when they might have realized at the same time that Las Vegas was known to be the capital of quickie weddings.

"It's from the hotel's chapel," Penn said slowly.

"Y-you have a chapel here?"

He winced. "Yeah, it was supposed to be ironic."

If this was real, it unfortunately might be extremely legal and binding. What would her family say about this? *You didn't have to sell your soul to get his business!* They'd never believe her if she told them she didn't remember marrying him. And the worst thing about all of this, the one thing her family would hang her for? There'd been no time for a prenup. Penn slid her a wary glance as if he'd realized the same thing. His family would also go ballistic. But who had time for a prenup when you didn't even realize what you were doing?

"Were we honestly *that* drunk?" she whispered.

He scrubbed a hand down his face. "Listen, I've got some bad news. I think we were exactly that drunk. Now that I'm fully alert, I remember getting our marriage license. I even have a faint recollection of picking out that ring in the gift shop downstairs."

Once he said the words out loud, Gia remembered, too, and cringed. She couldn't imagine what she'd been thinking. She and Penn barely knew each other. All that wine and the ability to get married too easily within a person's reach. The country should do something about this! Marriages were far too easy and accessible.

"So, this *is* real," she said sullenly. "But surely the officiant must have realized our inebriated state. They probably haven't mailed off the official paperwork yet, just in case we woke up and changed our minds! Right?"

"I hope you're right." Penn met her eyes. "And we can catch them before they do."

Penn dressed in record time, not bothering with a shower or shave. Every second was crucial. His watch told him it was already ten o'clock in the morning, so there was no time to waste. He barely had a moment to notice the soft curves of Gia's body as she dressed, but the overachiever in him managed anyway. No matter what else happened between them, he'd never regret last night. Memories of her flooded him, her sweet scent still lingering on him.

But he couldn't think about any of that right now. Her family was going to *kill* him. His family was going to *hate* her. People like them didn't get married like *this*. They had big, splashy weddings that were like corporate events—essentially, the parties of the year. His goal was to stop that marriage license from being filed with the great state of Nevada. After that, he would shut down that damn chapel.

Together, he and Gia met the cheerful attendant downstairs.

"Ah, here's the happy couple!" she exclaimed, arms wide open.

"You remember us?" Gia said.

"The officiant told me it was one of the most romantic and passionate weddings he's ever performed." She put a hand to her bosom. "You two recited *vows* to each other."

"Did they make *sense*?" Penn demanded. "Couldn't he tell we were drunk?"

"You were as capable as anyone else who walks through

these hallowed hallways." She crossed her arms and tipped her chin.

Penn quirked a brow. "And is that saying much?"

"He said you seemed *so in love*."

"Well, it sounds like you need a new officiant," Penn grumbled, gesturing between him and Gia. "We just met."

"Excuse me!" Gia interrupted. "It's awfully kind of you to remember our special day, but could you possibly let us see the license before you mail it off and make it official?"

"Yes," Penn said. "Give us the license. Now."

She pulled on his arm. "Penn, honey. I'm sure she's doing the best she can."

"I am." The attendant sniffed. "I always do."

"The license?" Gia said. *"Please?"*

She was gone two minutes. "This is our copy. The officiant was so excited to perform the ceremony for Penn Fortune himself that he dropped it off at the post office."

Penn felt his pulse skyrocket into triple digits. He glanced at Gia, who looked equally horrified, covering her mouth with her hand.

"What do you mean?" he said between gritted teeth.

"We're superefficient around here," she said. "I'm the manager."

"Why would you *do* that?" Penn pounded the counter. "That's over-the-top efficiency!"

"Thank you, I like to think so." She brightened and reached under the counter. "Oh, and here are the pictures from last night. They develop in an hour but you two didn't want to wait. I have a feeling you were, uh, anxious to consummate? Anyway, we have several wedding album packages available—"

Penn shook a finger. "No, thank you!"

The attendant pushed the envelope over and Gia took it from her. Penn was so furious he figured he better not touch anything less he break it.

"I'm closing this place down," Penn said, turning to leave. "No more quickie weddings on my watch!"

Remembering his manners, he opened the door of the chapel and led Gia—his *wife*—back to the bank of elevators leading to the penthouse.

"I'm sorry, Gia." He hung his head. "This is all my fault."

"How is this your fault?"

"Well, I have a *chapel* in my hotel, for one."

"And I didn't have to join you there in matrimony but obviously I did." She chuckled and shook her head. "Don't worry—we can have the marriage annulled when we get back to Emerald Ridge."

"Yeah, looks like that's the only option we have left at this point." He considered what had happened last night, beyond the wedding. "Are you okay? I mean, you know, everything else..."

"I'm fine. If I recall, our night together was mutual."

Penn felt a sense of relief flood him. He didn't want to take advantage of Gia and she'd been drunk. Then again, he'd been, too. They'd talked about it. Talked about being discreet and only temporary. But he'd never done anything like this before and didn't sleep around, choosing his partners carefully. The *last* thing he and his family needed was another scandal. He was also never going to be one of those men like his father, who strung women along and lied repeatedly.

"It was unforgettable. That's for sure." He smiled and put an arm around her for a sideways hug.

It was strange to have had this kind of connection and intimacy with someone he'd just met. Part of him wanted to ask for permission to touch her, to kiss her.

But if they were going to get this marriage annulled, it would be best not to have a repeat performance of last night.

Chapter Four

Back in Penn's living quarters, they took turns showering and dressing. He let Gia go first and made a valiant effort to look away from his *wife* when she emerged wearing only a towel wrapped around her luscious body. His wife. He would never get used to that word. It instituted full-on panic when it rolled around in his mind, so he certainly wasn't going to try it on his lips. Holy hell, he was a *husband.* That word wasn't any easier for his brain to accept.

"I left you some hot water," she said, brushing by him. "And I suppose I'll have to call for a car to get me to the airport. On top of everything else, I missed my flight."

"I'll take you back," he said. "I flew here yesterday—I have my own plane."

She quirked a brow. "I'm impressed."

"There's a lot about your husband you don't know." He flashed her a wink and didn't miss the way she blinked in surprise. "We may as well go back to Texas together."

Penn made a few business calls after he showered. Out of the corner of his eye, he caught Gia patiently waiting for him. He hated the cheap costume jewelry ring on her finger, which filled him with shame since he could have done much better. It didn't escape his notice that she was looking through the photo packet they'd been given. At least she wasn't crying, because he guessed this was *not* the way she'd imagined her first marriage. Usually, women wanted more from a wedding than just showing up, posing for a few photos and walking away with a ring. He did not want to see pictures of them both drunk and ridiculous, so he would not ask to see them.

He'd thought of something else earlier this morning, and though it might make awkward conversation, it needed to be discussed. It was possible they could wind up with an unplanned pregnancy in addition to an impromptu marriage.

"I meant to ask. I'm sorry but I don't think…did we use, you know, any protection?"

"There's nothing for us to worry about," she said, putting the photos away.

"Are you sure?"

"Yes," she repeated and wouldn't meet his eyes.

To him that meant she was on contraception. He was still mortified not to have used precautions and protected them both. It was not like him to be this reckless. But last night? His inhibitions had clearly been obliterated.

"You know, I don't do this. I don't sleep with someone I just met."

"Same." She met his eyes and he believed her.

He only hoped *she* believed him. Then his phone buzzed, getting his attention. He quickly scanned the message before turning back to Gia.

"The car's here to take us to the airport," Penn told her, grabbing his small overnight bag. "Ready?"

Ready or not, Gia was flying home with Penn. *On his private plane.* In case the small aircraft wasn't enough to wow her, he was also a trained pilot. Because she'd missed her early morning flight, she texted her sister and let her know she'd be in later than planned due to a mix-up at the airport.

Yeah, some mix-up. *Oops, I got married. Damn, I hate when that happens.*

She followed Penn up the small stairs. She'd been on small private planes, too, but none quite as glamorous as this one. The sleek interior had two white leather seats for passengers. It contained more space than she'd imagined. She settled down with her bag on one of the seats and watched as Penn made himself comfortable in the cockpit. He slipped on a headset and began speaking to someone over the intercom, going through his preflight check. Buttons were pushed and dials were flipped.

The engine roared to life, and he turned back, meeting her eyes. "You can sit up here with me if you'd like. It's just the two of us."

"Okay, thanks." Feeling more than a little bit intimidated by all the lights and controls, she settled into the seat next to him.

There's a lot you don't know about your husband, he'd said. Until that moment, she hadn't even applied that particular noun to him. On the one hand, their marriage still didn't seem real. On the other, the seal on the official certificate left no room for doubt. Then there were the photos. She'd been looking at them countless times, turning them over in her hands, slowly arriving at the acceptance this had *happened.* Seeing the pictures triggered memories from the night before, reinforcing that she hadn't been *that* drunk—just happy, apparently—smiling into the camera. Smiling at *Penn.* She hadn't looked that blissful since her sister Antonia's wedding.

But a quickie wedding in a Vegas chapel was not how she saw her wedding day going someday. She'd always wanted to be married outdoors, right on the vineyards of Leonetti land. Her parents, grandparents and great-grandparents were married there and all had long and blessed unions. She wanted that, too, with someone who loved her. Penn wanted children but didn't even believe in love *or* marriage. He had to be far more upset than she was about their nuptials, but except for the exchange with the manager of the chapel, he'd remained calm. When he'd asked about protection, which she read as obvious concern for an unplanned pregnancy, she didn't want to tell him she couldn't give him a baby even if she wanted to.

For many years, she'd suffered from painful menstruation and eventually been diagnosed with endometriosis. Her doctor warned she'd have a difficult, if not impossible, time getting pregnant. She wanted a child as badly as Penn did, but it would be far easier for him to do so with the right woman. Clearly, that couldn't be her. The smart thing to do was get the marriage annulled and thank goodness he agreed. This way, maybe she'd never even have to tell her family about this unfortunate mistake. Her brother, Leo, was a real tease, and if he found out, she'd never live it down.

Penn completed his preflight check, getting permission from the tower to take off. Soon they were passing over the city of Las Vegas with all the bustling activity below. To the west, the majestic peaks of the Sierras stood tall, the snow-capped mountains in the distance a spectacular sight.

"I've never sat in the cockpit before," Gia said. "You have the best seat in the house here."

He chuckled. "Every time I fly commercial, I realize how spoiled I am. Looking out a little window is not the same."

They settled into a quiet kind of ease and she studied Penn's profile. His strong jawline, full lips and straight nose. He would indeed make beautiful children and she hoped that for him someday. From everything she'd learned of Penn Fortune in the past few hours, she believed him to be a good man.

"How long have you been flying?"

"Well, my father was a pilot. He made his money owning airlines."

"This was something you two bonded over?"

His jaw tight, he nodded. "We did. I got my license when I was eighteen. From then on, I logged my flight hours. I begged people to be my passengers and let me fly them around. My brother, my mother, my classmates…"

"Your girlfriends?" she teased.

"Well, now that you mention it, I bought my first plane when I was twenty-five and *have* been known to whisk away a date to a restaurant in California that serves the best sushi. They have always been impressed."

"No wonder." She had a momentary pang of envy for those lucky women. "It's very romantic."

He shrugged. "I hope so."

They hadn't even been in the air an hour when Penn's entire demeanor changed. Gia saw the tension in his shoulders, the tightness in his jawline. When he began punching and flipping buttons, a sense of foreboding came over her.

"Is everything okay?"

He didn't answer for a full minute, his focus so intense. "We're getting close to the Rio Grande Valley near Albuquerque and the weather has shifted."

No sooner had he said that than the plane moved as if the wind itself had jostled it. Gia let out a sharp gasp when she felt the drop, but Penn remained cool.

"Unfortunately, it's beginning to look like these winds are only going to get worse. Possibly a monsoon is coming."

"A *monsoon*?"

Having lived in the Southwest all her life, Gia knew about monsoons. They meant torrential rain, winds and flooding but were rare enough she didn't spend any time worrying about them. At the moment, however, worry didn't even come close to capture what she was feeling.

Terrified was more like it.

Penn turned to her. "I'm going to make a forced landing."

Chapter Five

"You're going to land? *Where?*" Below, Gia saw nothing but empty space in big patches of agricultural land.

They must be miles from an airport, regional or otherwise.

"I studied the maps and there's a private airstrip below. Probably belongs to a rancher who has his own plane."

"Can you do that? Land there?" But the real question—the one she wouldn't voice out loud—was whether he had the skill required.

"Well, I better land or we'll fly right into that storm. Going around it at this point would mean wasting resources and more gas than I have."

"H-have you ever done a forced landing before?"

His jaw flexed before he answered. "I've never had to, but of course my training has given me all the knowledge."

Gia didn't find this terribly encouraging, but too distracted by the rain pelting down, she sat quietly as they flew ahead. Within minutes, she got a glimpse of ground down below.

"Hang on, Gia. Brace for landing."

Brace for landing? Those were three words she never thought she'd hear from anyone, least of all her accidental husband. She obeyed and tucked her body in as Penn began his descent on to what appeared to be an airstrip made out of dirt in the middle of nowhere. The rain and wind came down so hard now she doubted he could find it much less *land* near it. But Penn brought the plane down smoothly, applying the brakes as they skidded to a stop right before the strip ended.

When he cursed under his breath, Gia realized he, too, had been unnerved by this.

"Are you okay?" He stripped off his headset, unbuckled and knelt in front of her. "Tell me you're okay."

"Yes, yes. I'm fine." She let out a shuddering breath. "But that was *scary*."

"No kidding. For me, too." He raked a hand through his hair.

Penn helped her unbuckle and tugged on her hand to lead her to one of the better chairs in the passenger area of the plane. She should call her family to let them know this was more than a mix-up. When she pulled out her phone, she realized—not surprisingly—that she only had one bar. No Wi-Fi either, and they were stuck here in the middle of nowhere with no one to help.

"What do we do now?" Gia asked, as the wind and torrential rain rocked the plane every few minutes. "Just wait it out?"

He glanced at his watch. "I can't be sure how long this is going to last since it wasn't on any of the weather reports. It could be all night or be over in an hour. These sudden monsoons are unpredictable."

"All *night*?" She would have to sleep in this chair, which though comfortable, wasn't meant for that purpose.

"Yeah, but this wind worries me," Penn admitted as the plane rocked.

"So, what should we do?"

"We could stay in here but I'd feel better with some other type of shelter."

"Like what?" They were literally in a field probably miles away from civilization.

Penn begin to dig in a compartment and brought out a few items. "I have some rescue stuff here I've never used. *Always be prepared*. My dad taught me that. There's Mylar blankets in here and a sleeping bag."

He pulled out a jacket and put it on. "I'm going to see what I can find outside and be right back."

"What?" Gia stood. "You're going outside in *that*? No, Penn. It's too dangerous."

"I won't be long. If I can't find any shelter, I'll come right back."

"No," Gia pleaded, pulling on his hands. "Please don't leave me."

She was too embarrassed to admit this, but fear roiled through her at the thought of being out here alone in this storm. At least now when the plane swayed and rocked she had someone with her.

"Gia, honey. Look." He met her eyes, hands pressed on each of her shoulders. "My plane is built for aerodynamics. It's designed to be pushed around by the wind."

The realization hit her like a punch. "But it isn't safe to stay in here, is it? Even if we are on the ground."

He shook his head. "I'm afraid not. It's better than no shelter at all, but if this wind picks up anymore, we're likely to be tossed around."

"Oh, God."

"In fact," he said, shrugging out of his jacket and putting it on her. "Grab your bag. You're coming with me."

Penn said a quick prayer before he helped Gia climb out of the plane. Within seconds, they were assaulted by the pelting rain and winds. Holding her hand, he led her in the direction of the barn he'd seen from the air. Nothing fancy, he'd guess, but a solid structure built to withstand the wind. This wasn't a hurricane-level storm so it was something they'd have to wait out. And with any luck, if his plane was still there—and in one piece—after this, he'd fly them home. Maybe someday they'd actually joke about it.

Remember that time we got caught in a monsoon on our way back from our accidental wedding?

At the moment, however, he saw nothing funny about the way the rain hit him sideways so he could barely see a foot in front of him. He sensed Gia's hesitation and fear but she was being a good sport about this. Some of his ex-girlfriends would have already torn into him, berating him for the storm as if *he* controlled the weather. They'd complain about what it was doing to their hair and their shoes. Gia, on the other hand, was exactly the kind of woman he appreciated—someone who rolled with the punches. He'd been doing the same thing for most of his life.

Unexpectedly, the barn he'd seen turned out to be a cabin. With any luck, someone was here. Knocking, however, didn't get anyone's attention. Not even when he started to pound on the door. While Gia waited under the protection of a partial roof, Penn went around the back and stared inside the windows like a street urchin. This was humbling. Here he was, a hotelier with gobs of money at his disposal, and he might have to sleep in a plane that would blow around the field all night. Ironic.

The thing was, he would happily do that, and in fact didn't like leaving his plane. But he couldn't ask that of Gia. He *wouldn't.* Luck finally appeared in the form of an unlocked back door and Penn let himself in, hoping the owner wasn't in bed asleep with a rifle. Before he let Gia inside, he checked to be sure they were alone. He wandered through an empty back bedroom, dripping water all over the place, then the family room and kitchen. Cobwebs were everywhere he looked, a musty smell in the air.

He unlocked the front door and pulled Gia inside. "I've got good news and bad news."

"Are the people home?" She glanced around the cabin, probably taking in the lack of furnishings and coming to her own conclusions.

"The bad news is this cabin is abandoned. And the good news is this cabin is abandoned." With his hands, he started pulling away cobwebs. "We can stay here tonight if we have to."

"What are you doing? Why are you waving your arms around like that?"

He cleared his throat. "Don't panic, but there are a few spiderwebs here and there."

Here and there meant pretty much *everywhere* but he liked to break bad news slowly. Surprise turned to amusement when Gia joined him, brushing away the webs as they cleared the room to be suitable for human dwelling.

"You're not afraid of spiders?"

Every girl he'd ever dated would want to set this place on fire and sleep in a tree instead of a spider-infested cabin.

"Not me," she said, brushing her hands together. "A long time ago, my papa explained that I'm at least a hundred times bigger than any spider. They should be afraid of *me*."

"He was right." Penn chuckled. "I'm sorry, this is some honeymoon we're having."

"Now that I'm out of the wind and rain, I'm going to consider this a fun adventure. It's not like you planned it."

"No, the weather report didn't mention any precipitation," he agreed. "And let's face it, this weather is a rarity even in monsoon season."

At least they had a fireplace and could get warm. He

searched the house until he found a covered, dry wood pile—probably the original source of the spiders—on the outside wraparound deck. This cabin probably hadn't been abandoned long ago, as he found matches in a kitchen drawer. Unfortunately, no food, canned or otherwise. He couldn't have everything, he supposed, but a couch or bed with a few pillows might have been nice. If he didn't have the Mylar blankets and the sleeping bag they'd really be in trouble.

Penn hauled in a few logs and slowly piled them in the hearth. When he turned to get more, he found Gia right behind him, handing logs she'd carried in herself. She was walking a little funny and he remembered she'd been wearing heels. *Past tense.* One was cut off, the other still working. She hadn't mentioned it once. Still, they were a team, working together under the least pleasant circumstances he'd personally ever experienced.

"This is a bit like camping," Gia said. "Don't you think?"

He shot her a curious look, intrigued. "Did you do much of that as a kid?"

"Papa took us all the time when we were growing up. But mostly, we camped on our own vineyard. He would put up a tent and try to make it like the real thing, with sleeping bags, flashlights and s'mores." A small laugh escaped her. "But our main house was only a few yards away. Leo and I loved it more than my sisters did. They would always run back to our mother and ask to sleep in their own beds. But me, I loved being next to my father in my cozy sleeping bag."

"What would he think of this? One sleeping bag and two blankets. This is really roughing it. At least for us."

Gia shook her head and finally kicked off her shoes. "Nah. I bet Papa is looking down from heaven now, having a good laugh."

Penn didn't know her father was dead. "When did he die?"

"Ten years ago." She handed Penn another log. "It was a rough time. I was getting ready to go to college but I didn't want to leave my mother, so I took a gap year. She took his death hard. He was the love of her life."

Penn thought back to his mother's grief at losing her husband, and how that grief turned to confusion and anger at his betrayal. He couldn't imagine finding that someone you loved for decades had such deep, dark secrets.

"Ever since she lost my father, she hasn't wanted much to do with the family business," Gia went on to say. "I think it's too painful not to see my father out there, tending the vines, keeping track of the weather. He was old-school about all that and liked doing it himself, even when we got to the point where he didn't have to."

Penn nodded silently, then struck a match and hoped for the best. A little paper or kindling would be a godsend, but beggars couldn't be choosers. As if she'd heard him, Gia pulled some papers out of her bag and handed them over.

She shook her head when he sent her a questioning look. "Use it. Just a few notes I don't need."

The flame caught the papers on fire and they were in business.

"And it's still family-run even if your mother wants no part of it, right?"

"Remember I said my papa was old-school? Well, after his death, the company was handed over to our brother, Leo. It should have gone to Bella, who's always been the most interested in the field and the expert on grapes. But for my father, it made sense for Leo to take charge. He didn't necessarily want it."

Gia fanned her hands in front of the fire for warmth and kept talking.

"Bella thought our father chose Leo based on his gender

rather than birth order. Unfortunately, I think that was true. It was not a fun time when all that happened, but they've worked it out. Leo made Bella head vintner when Papa's right-hand man retired. She's the expert on making the wine—I'm the expert at selling it." She touched her breast with a hint of pride.

"The baby of the family, huh? They say the youngest in a family can sell sand in the desert. Is that true about you?" He winked.

"I guess so, but truthfully sometimes I wish Bella would involve me more in the tending of the grapes. I'd love to be more involved in the soup to nuts process but I don't want to encroach on Bella's territory." Her cheeks pinked a little and when he took a good long look at her, he realized she was shivering.

"You're *freezing*," Penn said, standing and pulling her toward him. "Here, get in front of the fire. In a minute it will be roaring and give us some heat."

He removed his sopping wet jacket off her, scolding himself for not having done this sooner. If he was cold, he had to assume it would be far worse for her. He opened the boxes that contained the Mylar blankets and sleeping bag. Since ordering them a year ago, he hadn't even opened them but found comfort in the fact they were there if needed. Now he cursed himself for only having one sleeping bag. If they had to share it, they'd certainly be *cozy* tonight.

He handed Gia an emergency blanket. "You should take off all your clothes."

Chapter Six

"And get warm, I mean," Penn said, in case Gia thought this was his unorthodox way of seducing her. Again. "Our clothes are soaking wet and it will be tougher to get warm while still wearing them."

She stared at the blanket, then at him. "You're right."

"I won't look," Penn promised, turning and giving her his back.

"It's not like you haven't already seen everything there is to see," she muttered and out of the corner of his eye, he saw her pants drop to the dusty wooden floor, followed closely by her underwear. His heart rate kicked up because he couldn't help wanting to see more of his wife.

Penn also kicked off his shoes, pants and shirt, and then bent to open the second box with the Mylar blanket. Nothing fancy, and it crinkled as he put it around himself. It was silver and shiny and reminded him of the space station. Once, he'd told his father he wanted to be an astronaut, proving he'd always had an affinity for flying.

"You can't be an *astronaut*," he'd said. "You're going to run my company someday."

Way to squash a seven-year-old's dream. He probably would have changed his mind anyway at some point, especially after learning of the stringent requirements and the education involved. But if only he'd known at the time, he could've told his father: *"Get one of your other kids to run your company."* But as far as Penn knew back then, he and Hayes were his only children. And his brother had always loved the rodeo, a different kind of flying.

Penn hung their clothes on hooks that probably once held hats and jackets. He tried to picture who might have lived here. Maybe a small family, a couple just starting out, or perhaps a lone bachelor who'd never found anyone to marry.

Penn joined Gia by the fire, where she sat with her red painted toenails sticking out from beneath the blanket. He tried desperately not to picture her naked body under there. True, he'd already seen everything and *every* part was memorable. He'd be a lucky man to be with her again.

"Thanks for all your help," he said thickly. "You're being a really good sport about all this."

"I'm not the type to stand around and watch others work. My parents taught me to take care of myself and always help others."

"It shows." Telling himself that she'd get warmer faster with him close, he edged near her so their blankets touched. "We make a great team, but I would imagine you'd make a great partner to anyone."

She nodded and smiled.

He liked her so much that a part of him wondered if they should *stay* married. Maybe their accidental marriage was a blessing in disguise. In his situation, an arrangement like this was ideal. He didn't want to fall in love, didn't need all those intense and messy complications. Romantic entanglements always seemed to end in pain.

What he wanted was a partner. Someone to help him raise a family. Children.

Gia wanted a family, too. Staying together could work—a union between two wealthy families. No mess, no heartbreak.

His mother would probably perform a soft shoe dance at the news.

It was up to him to present this suggestion to Gia like a business opportunity. He wasn't in marketing, but he had skills of his own.

"I've been thinking and I have an idea," Penn said. "Why don't we *forgo* the annulment?"

Gia couldn't have heard Penn right. The fire was roaring and a branch crackled and split, not to mention the storm raging outside.

"What did you say?"

"I'm thinking that it's not a bad idea for us to stay married. You and me." He gestured between them. "Think about it. We make sense. We're the same age, with similar values. I want a partner, and I think you do, too."

"Yes, but—"

"Hear me out. Granted, I'm not a born salesperson like you are, but I think I can make you an attractive proposition."

She quirked a brow. He must be *joking.* "You already did, given I woke up next to you this morning."

Penn chuckled. "True, but I'm talking about something much bigger. A *legacy.* I'm talking about a future and giving each other the family we both want."

A sharp pain sliced through her at the thought of children. She'd told him she wanted a child, but he didn't know she couldn't have one. In her last relationship, she was so certain she and Marco would be together forever that she'd been careless about protection. Every single time she was fine, never pregnant. She recalled another pregnancy "scare" early in her life, which had resulted in nothing. At the time, she'd been happy and relieved. But after a few oopses and no baby, after a while, she'd started to wonder if she had a problem.

Memories of her ex's last words to her after she broke up with him still rang in her ears.

"You shouldn't be so picky, Gia. When a woman can't have children, no man is going to want her long-term."

She didn't want to believe it to be true, and her sisters continually reminded her that she could adopt. Gia wasn't averse to the idea, but she couldn't help feeling her body had betrayed her by not giving her this most basic function. She'd bet that Penn wanted a biological child, too, considering his family scandal. Somewhere there was a man who didn't care but that wouldn't be Penn Fortune.

"I couldn't be part of a marriage that isn't based on true love," she said after several seconds of silence.

He stared at the fire's flickering flames. "You wouldn't even *consider* staying married to me? I think we're well suited for each other."

"We're not, Penn."

He turned to her, confusion clouding his green eyes. "Why would you say that?"

She covered her face with her hands. He didn't need to know this about her—the *real* reason they would never work. But considering they were already married, he would probably never give up trying to convince her they belonged together unless she told him the truth.

She felt exposed in so many ways. It wasn't because of her naked body beneath the metallic blanket shimmering like a disco ball, but because of her *heart*, already beginning to open to Penn. He wasn't chasing fairy tales—that much was clear. Her *husband* had a mission: to build a family while steering clear of love. She was the wrong person for him in that way, too. Someday she'd find the man who didn't care she might not be able to give him biological children, but that would require a deep love connection, and Penn didn't even *want* to get there.

"I'd disappoint you in the first few months of our marriage."

"I doubt that very much." He reached over to lower her hands from her face and met her eyes, his gaze tender. "I've already said you're a good partner, both in business and in marriage. When you really put it down to basics, marriage is a contract and nothing more."

"You have a heartless way of looking at marriage, then," Gia huffed.

"Not heartless, but practical. Look at my family, for example. I thought we were *normal*. I believed my parents adored each other, but my father had two other families."

"I'm sorry that happened to you, but I have problems of my own." Her voice broke. "We wouldn't make a good partnership even if I was willing to overlook the fact that you don't want a marriage that could lead to love. I—I can't have children."

To her horror, Gia burst into tears. She'd thought she'd have better control over her emotions, but she couldn't hold back.

Wiping away her tears, she sobbed, "I'm sorry."

Penn pulled her into his arms, which meant they were now sharing a blanket between them. "Don't be sorry, sweetheart. *I'm* the one who's sorry. I can't believe I brought this up—"

"You didn't know, it's not your fault." His warm, taut skin pressed against hers, giving her a sense of calm and security amid this raging storm. "I might never be a mother…"

She loved his natural scent and buried her face in his chest. This was a man she could easily fall for, but while he had such soulless opinions on marriage, she wouldn't allow herself to. It meant nothing but agony to love a man who could never love her in return.

As he held her close, Penn's breath fanned against her temple. "The truth is, I more than most people understand family means a lot more than DNA. When I was a teenager, I overheard my mother talking on the phone, saying she worried Hayes might not be my father's son. I guess she'd had an affair around the time of his conception."

Gia blinked, stunned. Hearing this now, even she had to admit it explained a lot—the walls he'd erected around his heart. With so many red flags in his past, it made sense Penn was disillusioned with the idea of a loving marriage.

"Anyway, after Archibald died—and all these other wives and half siblings came out of the woodwork, wanting their share of the Fortune dynasty—I didn't want to have anything to do with it. But according to the terms of the will, if we don't find all the siblings, then *no one* gets an inheritance." He sighed, his body tensing for just a moment before he continued. "I'd moved to Houston, and frankly, I was worried we'd find out Hayes was only my half brother if he took a DNA test. It would affect his inheritance. But in fact, it never mattered to me. He's still my brother, always has been and always will be no matter the biology."

"I've never met a man quite like you."

"They broke the mold after God made me." Penn chuckled. "The truth is, I have a colorful family history. If it won't bore you, I'll tell you about it."

"Please," Gia said softly into his chest. "We're not going anywhere for a while."

Outside, the wind howled and beat against the windows and shutters. The rain continued to pelt down, the scent of wood and pine filling the small cabin.

"With my father's death, we've learned a lot more about the Fortunes. My grandparents, Clyde and Cass, actually died penniless when my father was fourteen. Apparently, they'd owned a small parcel of land near the tracks that foreclosed sixty years ago, yet somehow Archibald emerged from that impoverished situation already wealthy in his early twenties. No one has any idea what happened to him during those missing years."

"How did he make all his money?" Gia wondered. "And he was so young, too."

"No one knows," Penn replied "But that's just one of the mysteries we're going to unravel through our investigation."

"You're right. It's an interesting history."

"Interesting? That's a kind word for it." He snorted. "*Scandalous* is a better one. So, you see, Gia, it would be asking a lot from *you* to hitch your wagon to mine, so to speak."

"Is that right, cowboy?" Gia chuckled.

"I'd be extremely lucky if you would consider staying married to me." With that, he kissed her bare shoulder, which sent a tremble through her that had nothing to do with the cold.

Chapter Seven

Once nightfall arrived and the storm still raged, Penn accepted they would have to stay the night. After hours of a fire, they'd burned all the logs. Everything else would be too wet to burn. Either way, it was time to break out the sleeping bag. He guessed that after turning down his idea to stay married, Gia wouldn't be thrilled about sharing it with him. He reached for the box, which had the new sleeping bag in it, and pulled it out. Also made from Mylar, the shiny silver brightened up the room, like having their own moon in this cabin.

"Since it looks like we'll be here all night…you should know I only have one sleeping bag."

"Just one?" She eyed the bag. "Oh boy, that looks…too small for both of us."

"It will keep us warm. This was my emergency stash and I hadn't expected to be stranded with company. If there's ever a next time, I'll make sure to have two." He laid the bag in front of the dwindling fire. "I'm afraid we're going to have to share. If you don't mind…"

She shook her head. "That's okay. It will be good for body heat because it's going to be a long and cold night."

Again, she hadn't disappointed him with her ability to accept things were not going to be ideal. This wasn't a six-star resort.

"Speaking of sharing." She pulled out a wrapped granola bar from her bag "Here's dinner."

"You big spender," Penn deadpanned, taking his half and devouring it in two bites.

He had forgotten how low the temperatures could get in parts of New Mexico.

"Here, you climb in first," he gestured.

Gia complied, still using her blanket for cover.

"The blanket will make a good pillow," he said.

"Good idea." She folded it and packed it under her head.

Now she was completely naked under the sleeping bag. He should have suggested they dress, but the clothes weren't dry enough yet. Penn swallowed hard and dropped his own blanket to climb in. But clearly, this wasn't going to work. Gia was right—even a large sleeping bag was too small for two people. He tried not to squish and pin her down.

"I think you should have gotten in first," Gia informed him. "I'm smaller."

"Right," Penn said, but he was already in the bag, so he rolled to shift their positions.

"Ouch!" Gia yelped when he elbowed her.

"Sorry," he said, because of the elbow and also a certain part of his anatomy that had decided it was about to have a fun time. *Wrong.*

Another roll and Gia wound up on top of him. She smiled down at him, her long, dark hair like a curtain between them.

"What a view," he murmured. "Do you think you could just sleep on top of me all night?"

He was only half kidding.

"No, I'm sorry." Then she lowered herself to his side, nestling into the crook of his arm.

"Unfortunately, now we've managed to roll ourselves too far from what's left of the fire."

Her head peeked out. "Yikes. You're right."

"Let's just work together and inch our bodies back."

They did just that, grunting and moving like one big giant worm.

Gia laughed. "Too bad I was never good at the worm dance."

"You're talking to the worm *champ*," Penn boasted. "I used to entertain all my friends."

By the time they were adjusted, they were both laughing and out of breath.

"We're such a pair," Gia said, now more comfortably settled in the crook of his arm.

"If only our families could see us now," Penn chuckled, brushing a kiss on her shoulder.

"Well, we're legally sanctioned," Gia reminded him. "In the state of Nevada."

"In all states," Penn corrected.

They were both quiet for several seconds.

"I want you to know," Gia whispered, "even if it was an accident, I'm never going to regret you being my first husband. No matter how long this marriage lasts, it's going to be tough to beat the standard you've set for adventure and fun."

The thought of any other man with Gia was a gut punch. He didn't want anyone even trying to compete with him for Gia.

"You're not disappointed that we're not staying in the honeymoon suite at one of my fancy hotels?"

"With a heart-shaped tub?" She rolled her eyes. "That sounds kind of hokey and boring, actually."

"Hell, no. I refused to have the heart-shaped tubs in my hotels. And it's *official*—you're unlike any woman I've ever met."

"Because I don't miss the fancy stuff? My father was basically a farmer. Yes, a wealthy one, but we know how to make do with what we have. The Leonettis always have."

"You're making a strong case for my dream woman. Can't I convince you to stay hitched?" His lip quirked up in a smile. "This doesn't have to stay an accidental marriage. That's entirely up to you."

"You *still* want to stay married even knowing I can't ever have a baby?"

"Absolutely. We could always adopt or use a surrogate. There are options."

"I didn't think you were serious about that. There are other choices but it gets…complicated."

"Listen. I don't *care*. You and I would raise great kids. I know it. Even without a marriage based on love."

"Penn, thank you for that. It means a lot." She was quiet for so long he thought she'd fallen asleep, until she spoke in a whisper so faint he strained to hear it. "But sorry, my answer's still no. I won't stay married to someone whose heart is closed to love."

He was ready to say, "Give me half a chance," but he understood her point.

She wanted true love—and he didn't have it in him to offer that. Not to her, not to anyone.

For the second morning in a row, Gia woke up next to Penn. Except this time, she was pretty much plastered to his flesh in this tiny sleeping bag. Between their body heat and the bag, she'd started to sweat.

Outside, she heard birds chirping and…silence. The wind and rain had passed.

Gia desperately wanted a shower and a change of clothes. She would have to dress in yesterday's outfit and her broken, muddy heels. Even so, when it came to husbands, though she had nothing to compare, Penn set the bar high. If only he believed that marriage was more than a contract. His beliefs were understandable but not in line with hers. Funny, they didn't go along with everything else she'd learned about the man. But she would not compromise on this. She'd been fooled once before; thought a man loved her when he only loved her money. At least Penn was honest. She had to give him that.

"Good morning," she said, when Penn moved.

He groaned and dragged a hand down his face. "Morning."

"It stopped raining."

"Good. Let's get out of here." He unzipped the bag, and climbed out—buck naked—and found their clothes, throwing hers over.

He was so at ease naked and why not? He had an incredible physique, rock-strong arms and abs that made her weak. Seeing him naked for only the second time made her wish for a third even if it probably wouldn't, and couldn't, happen.

She caught her panties midair. "So…*not* a morning person?"

Yesterday, he'd been pulled out of a deep sleep and had good reason to be grumpy. Today, she couldn't say why he was so upset when they could now go home.

"Not really," he said, shrugging into his button-up. "But that's not it. I deserve a medal for not touching you all night long."

She blinked. "Excuse me? We couldn't have been any closer. You *touched* me all night long."

"Not the way I wanted to," he muttered, zipping up his pants. "I'm a damn saint."

That made her smile because she'd had some of the same thoughts last night. But with his talk of marriage and contracts, she didn't want to get any more addicted to Penn. If he needed signals from her, she'd been careful not to send them.

"I'll ask my mother to write to the Vatican and have you canonized. But you need three miracles."

He scowled. "The first was landing the plane on a dirt airstrip in the middle of nowhere."

"Good point, although that *could* be called skill. You'll need a third miracle and then you're in business."

Fully dressed, blankets folded and holding her briefcase, Gia tried to slip on her heels, wondering if she could cut off the other heel so they'd match. She still had to walk to the airplane through a muddy field and hoped it hadn't been pushed far by the storm last night.

She held up the shoe. "Do you think there's a way…?"

Penn grabbed the shoes and threw them in the fireplace. "I'll buy you a new pair. I can't stand to watch you hobble around in those."

"Why did you do that? I still have to—"

But without another word, Penn swept her up in his arms and carried her to the door. He kicked it open. "We forgot to do this. Aren't you supposed to carry your wife across the threshold?"

"If you slipped into a time machine and went back to the 1950s."

"Guess I'm old-fashioned."

They found the plane not far from where they'd left it, and after checking mechanics carefully, Penn performed his third miracle: he used a wet airstrip and somehow still got them airborne.

Once they were close to Texas, Gia's phone started seizing with multiple texts from Antonia, Leo and Bella. She read Bella's frantic note.

Where are you? Your plane was supposed to have landed yesterday! I checked the news and no accidents reported. You better respond soon or Mama will call the FBI.

Gia quickly replied: Long story. Tell you when I get home, but I'm fine and will be at the office shortly.

Bella instantly wrote back: Thank God! How did it go with the infamous Penn Fortune? Did he bite your head off and feed you to the wolves?

Really good. I made friends with him. He's going to carry our wines in his hotels.

She paused, finger hovering over the keyboard. *Best not to tell Bella that she'd married the man.*

Setting her phone down, she studied Penn's profile—once again the picture of calm concentration. "We haven't decided what, or if, we're going to tell our families about our marriage," she said quietly.

"It's probably not something we have to do if you *insist* on annulling our marriage."

He sounded irritated, but seriously, what did he expect? She'd already made herself clear: If he wanted her to stay married to him, she might need a little bit of romance. A little love. Good grief…she didn't want him to *fake* being in love with her, but he should at least be open to the possibility.

"Then I guess we shouldn't tell anyone," Gia said.

"Great."

It would be difficult to keep the truth from her family because they were so close, but she would do what she had to do. She'd hide the photos of their wedding at the chapel in her safe at the office. A truth she didn't want to examine too closely was that she didn't *want* to get rid of them. They were memories, like all others, and deserved respect. Someday, if she ever got married again, she'd shred them. Or she'd give them to Penn, who by then might be married to someone else he didn't love.

She'd say, "Remember when we got married that time?"

"Don't tell my wife," he'd joke.

"But I was your first," she'd say. "It just didn't stick."

For some reason, the thought brought tears to her eyes.

Chapter Eight

The rest of the flight went smoothly since they were thirty minutes from Texas by air. Penn landed at the regional airport in Emerald Ridge where a car waited for them. As instructed by Penn before they left Vegas, the driver had picked up Gia's luggage on the earlier flight, which had ridden in the baggage compartment alone. Now, she pulled out another pair of shoes from her suitcase.

"I'm sorry about throwing your shoes in the fireplace," Penn said.

"You sure are grumpy in the morning. But it's not like I wanted to keep them. They were ruined." She squeezed his forearm because he sounded so contrite. "I forgive you."

He slid her an easy smile, his eyes crinkling. "You would."

"I had a good time, despite all the, um, complications." She threw a look in the direction of the driver.

Penn rolled up the privacy divider. "We did have a few." He took her hand. "Will you at least think about it? Staying married to me?"

"Oh, Penn..." She could tell how much he wanted this, and this man tempted her beyond reason—but she couldn't hang her future on someone who didn't believe in love.

Yes, love was messy and *complicated*, but so were all the best things in life. She wished he could see that.

Penn brought her hand to his lips and brushed a kiss across

her knuckles. "Why not take a few days to consider it?" he said gently. "We'll have to wait until the marriage certificate arrives in the mail to apply for the annulment anyway."

Gia bit her lip, mulling it over. Truth was, she was so drawn to him she could barely think straight. She couldn't *breathe*.

He had good intentions—she honestly believed that—but how long could he stay faithful and loyal to someone he didn't love? But maybe…if they spent some time together as husband and wife, he might develop real feelings for her. He could change his mind about love.

Right?

And if it didn't work, they could still annul. There was no rush. She didn't have anything to lose by waiting a week to see how things went.

"Okay."

"Yeah?"

The smile he gave her sent a kick straight to her heart.

"Let's give it a week. It can't hurt to think about getting out of this a bit more carefully than we got *into* it." She quirked a brow.

"Good point. I can't ask for more than that."

Penn's car service dropped her off at her condo downtown, and finally home, Gia had a long, luxurious shower. She dried and styled her hair, dressed in clean clothes and headed to the vineyard offices downtown for a day of work. Now that she had so many new clients in Las Vegas, and particularly Fortune Resort Hotel, there was plenty of follow-up to do. She would have to check inventory, schedule a timeline for deliveries and contact all the appropriate personnel.

Anything to get her mind off the mess she'd made in Vegas.

She found Bella waiting behind Gia's desk, arms folded, an expectant smile on her face. She was dressed in her usual uniform of overalls and boots, always more comfortable among the vines than people.

"Hey! Welcome home, you rock star." Bella spun around on the swivel chair. "Why the hell are you so late?"

Gia wanted to tell her sister everything, how she'd married Penn Fortune, a serious catch. He was one of the most eligible bachelors in Emerald Ridge, and a bachelor no longer. But she couldn't tell Bella. She'd worry too much about Gia, not to mention question the sanity of such a quickie marriage. And there was the whole lack of a prenup thing. Leo would have a *fit*. If they stayed married and then later ended up getting divorced, Penn could force them to sell the vineyard to get his half of Gia's inheritance. But he wouldn't. The Fortunes had more money than they could ever spend in one lifetime.

"Penn offered to fly me home on his private plane," Gia explained. Best of all, it was not a lie. "So I took him up on it. I canceled my flight and got a credit."

"Tell me all about it." Bella stood and walked over to Gia. "Did he drool over my wine?"

Her sister had a proprietary take on their wine, like they were more of her children, and Bella already had two kids from a previous marriage.

"It was a great trip, for the most part," Gia replied. "Did you tell Leo and Antonia about Fortune Hotel yet?"

"No, I thought you might have. You mean for once *I* know something before they do?"

"I didn't get a chance to talk to them after my meeting with Penn, just right before."

"They're in a meeting right now, but I'll let them know you're in." Bella brushed by Gia on the way out. "I'll be in the casking room out at the vineyard if anyone needs me."

"Oh, and by the way," Gia said quickly, catching her before she left. “I’m going to need a case of that new cabernet for myself. It’s incredible.”

Bella grinned, hand in the pockets of her overalls. “Il mio vino é il tuo vino.”

My wine is your wine.

While that was true, Gia didn’t know a grape from a bean in the way Bella did. Only Bella could make the grapes sing the same way Papa had. It would be nice if Bella would take Gia under her wing and include her more in the process, but so far she didn’t seem to want anyone else involved.

Once Gia finally sat to make a few phone calls—thinking of her handsome husband the entire time—she couldn’t stand it a moment longer. She had to tell *someone*.

Gia pressed the intercom. “Adele, could you come in here for a sec?”

Adele Lorenzo was arguably Gia’s best friend. They’d gone to school together, and when Adele came back to Texas after college, Gia had given her a job as her personal assistant.

In two seconds, Adele was in the office. “Hey! How did it go? I heard you didn’t make your flight.”

Gia made a gesture for the woman to shut the door.

She did, eyes wide. “What happened?”

“First, I spent last night in a cabin because of a monsoon,” Gia said.

“What?!”

“Yes, I was on a private plane with Penn Fortune and he had to do a forced landing in the middle of nowhere. I was so scared!”

“Oh my gawd.”

“We found an empty, spider-infested cabin and spent the night there.”

“Did you say *spiders*?” Adele brought her hand to her neck.

Apparently, she didn't have the same level of acceptance for them Gia did.

"But that's not the most important part." Gia cleared her throat. "I got married."

"What?" her bestie squealed. "Why would you get married during a monsoon? What's *wrong* with you?"

"I'm getting ahead of myself." She waved her hand. "Not during the monsoon. Before, when I was in Vegas."

"I didn't even know you were back together with Marco!"

"No, not Marco." Gia shook her head and stood, coming around from behind her desk.

She'd never miss that man again. Not when Penn wanted to *stay* married to her. There was a new bar when it came to men and it was too high for Marco to ever reach.

"Have you been holding out on me?" Adela put her hand to her hip. "Who did you marry and why wasn't I invited?"

"Penn Fortune," Gia said and watched as Adele's jaw went slack.

"Are you *kidding* me?"

"You can't tell anyone! Especially not my family." Gia grabbed Adele by both shoulders and gave her a little shake.

"How's that going to work?"

Clearly, it wasn't *ever* going to work. But for now, it would have to be this way until they decided whether or not to annul.

"Because it was an accident. I might not stay married." With that, Gia dug in her bag for the photos and put them on her desk. "We'll probably get it annulled."

Then she told Adele everything, feeling her body shrink as she tried to explain the unexplainable.

Overwhelmed, her friend plopped down on the chair like all the air had been let out of her. "Oh, yikes! You hear about this kind of thing happening but…to you?"

"I blame Bella's new cabernet. It went down so smooth I

honestly didn't feel like I was drinking wine. The next thing you know, I'm waking up married."

Adele reached for the photos and began to flip through them. "How sweet! Look at you two, you look *so* happy."

"We were apparently quite drunk."

"And yet you're both standing and looking sharp in these pictures. When I'm drunk I might have sexy times without thinking it all the way through, but *marriage*? I mean, what got you *there*?"

Adele made a good point. They'd gone through a few steps to get *there*, which meant maybe deep down this was something they both wanted. People said inhibitions were lowered with alcohol, so maybe true desires were revealed, too. Gia could see why their marriage made sense in a logical way. But getting married the way they had suggested there was no logic behind it. Possibly only deep-seated desires.

"I don't know..."

"I do," Adele said confidently. "I mean, take Penn for instance. He's a real catch. And then, take a look at you. What man *with a pulse* wouldn't want you?"

Spoken like a best friend.

"Marco, for one." And any other man who wanted a biological child of their own.

"Marco is a *jerk*."

"I told Penn I can't have children, and he's okay with that, too."

Hearing him say those words, she hadn't realized how much it meant to her to know he wanted *her*.

"Oh my God, honey." Adele came close and gave Gia a much-needed hug. "That's a *real* man. Don't you dare throw him away."

"I know, he's pretty great." Gia's breath hitched. "No wonder I married him. But the problem is he wants a marriage in name only. No love. Like a business arrangement."

"You could change his mind. Call him, right now." Adele demanded, pulling away to hand Gia the phone.

"What? Why?" She looked at the phone as if it were a snake.

"Ask him out on a date. You need to get to know this man, spend some time with him. Then you'll see if this could ever work."

But what if Gia managed to fall in love with him in a week, and he didn't fall for her?

Chapter Nine

Back in the offices of Fortune Resorts later that morning, Penn couldn't stop thinking about Gia. The reality that he was married kept circling in his mind. No ring on his finger…and he should probably do something about that. He was someone's *husband.* And Penn, who never took responsibilities lightly, was already taking his role as Gia's husband seriously. Maybe he should look into changing his beneficiary or adding her to his health insurance policy. But he shouldn't get too excited. She hadn't agreed to stay married—yet. He'd have to work on her, because she'd given them a chance.

One week.

Basically, one week for him to get her to see he could give her a good life. For her to see and understand that marriage was literally a contract between two people. Love didn't need to be a part of that equation. For him, a bonus would be spending every night in bed with Gia…surely she would allow that. For the first time in his life, he'd have a real partner, someone smart he could bounce ideas off. Someone in his corner. But one week wasn't much time, so he'd have to get on this.

For starters, he needed a ring. A *spectacular* ring. He'd given her costume jewelry because it had been available, but she needed something classy and gorgeous. Like Gia. This would demonstrate how seriously he took their marriage. The problem was, he couldn't tell anyone in his family or get any advice. Otherwise, he'd hit up Hayes and ask him if his fiancée, Flora, would go with him to get the right piece. He didn't know one diamond set from the other but understood this was important to women. Of course, Gia wasn't *most* women, one of the things he liked best about her. He still wasn't going to shortchange her in the ring department, though.

His intercom buzzed and his assistant spoke. "Line 1. It's Gia Leonetti for you."

Gia. Holy shit. Did she miss him or had she already changed her mind? More than likely, it was the latter. Maybe he should avoid her so she couldn't break it off this soon. He could have his assistant tell her he was in a meeting. She needed to give him half a chance.

Okay, Penn. C'mon, you coward. Pick up the damn phone.

"Hey," he said, wincing and bracing himself for bad news. "Are you okay?"

"Yes. I was thinking that we—"

"Gia, look. Give us a chance. That's all I'm asking. It hasn't been a day much less a week."

She laughed. "Calm down. I'm calling to ask you out on a date. Is that okay?"

He almost laughed out loud in relief. "That's a great idea. What about this Friday, seven o'clock? Let me do the planning."

"Sure, that's fine with me." She hesitated a moment and then spoke again. "I can't wait to see you."

"Me, too."

They had so much to discuss. How this would work and how they'd manage life as business partners.

Excitement was a small word for the way Penn felt, like everything he'd ever wanted could fall into place for him. All this, at a time of chaos in his family, was exactly what he needed. Someone real and genuine like Gia who with her intelligence and wit would see the logic in this arrangement once she got past her previous ideas about marriage.

He tried to work for the next hour but couldn't concentrate.

"I'm going out on an errand," Penn said to his assistant. "Be back in a while. If anyone needs me, I have my cell."

He had an elaborate date to plan, and that's where he'd give Gia the ring. Maybe once he slipped it on, this marriage would feel real to her. She'd see the gesture as loving and significant. He did not understand her insistence there be romantic love in a marriage but maybe he could get her past that antiquated idea. The important thing in a marriage was two people who were compatible and wanted all the same things. Okay, maybe it wasn't romantic, but people in other cultures did this sort of thing all the time—an arranged marriage for practical reasons—and it worked out exceedingly well.

On his way to the jewelry store, Penn stopped at the Coffee Connection. This morning he'd had no time for coffee and the headache from caffeine withdrawal had started to hit him. It was probably another reason he'd been so grumpy this morning. That, and the fact he'd slept all night next to Gia and never made a move on her. He'd waited hours for a signal, something, *anything*, but when nothing came, he'd fallen asleep, unable to keep his eyes open anymore.

As usual, the shop was filled with the aroma of freshly brewed coffee and pastries. There were sofas filled with pillows, students and businesspeople sitting in front of their laptops. Penn walked up to the long bar by the counter and placed his order. He saw Madeline sitting on one of the overstuffed sofas nursing a coffee, scrolling through her phone, and decided he should check in with his half sister. He heard she'd gotten engaged recently to Forrest Porter, an architect and land developer with two young children.

"Hey, there, I hear congratulations are in order."

She sat up straighter and put her phone away. "Yes! Finally, he got wise and put a ring on it."

"He's a smart man."

Madeline beamed. "So, what's new with you?"

I got married to the most gorgeous woman I've ever met. Nope, can't talk about that yet.

"Yesterday I had to land my plane somewhere in the middle of New Mexico during a flash monsoon. That was fun."

"*What?* Oh Penn, thank goodness you're okay!"

"It would have meant splitting our father's inheritance with one less share," he joked.

Madeline didn't find it funny and scowled. "I value you more as a brother than I do whatever *shares* you own."

"Sorry, not funny." Penn shook his head. "Do me a favor and don't mention the airplane thing around my mother. She already hates me flying."

Madeline held a finger to her lips. "Don't worry, I know how moms can be. I won't say a word. Any news from the PI on our missing brother?"

"I just got an update from the PI. Nothing. I wish I had better news. It takes time when people use aliases, but eventually we'll track him down and make the connection."

Madeline was more eager than most to find their brother. She seemed to thrive on suddenly having siblings in her life since she'd been raised an only child. And curiosity, more than anything else, drove Penn. He had another brother out there somewhere.

"I'm sorry to always ask about this every time I see you. The not knowing is so frustrating. We have a *brother* out there." Something caught her eyes and Madeline looked over his shoulder. "Isn't that the woman from the vineyard in town? I took a tour last month."

Penn's heart rate kicked up as he turned to see Gia in line.

She looked beautiful, having changed into a dress and a new pair of heels that accentuated her luscious legs.

"Yes, that's Gia Leonetti of Leonetti Vineyards."

My wife. He waved her over and she joined them.

"Hi, Madeline," Gia said then turned to Penn with a smirk. "Hello, Penn. It's been a while."

"I thought that was you," Madeline said, standing. "I enjoyed my tour of Leonetti Vineyards last month. I really need to go again. They're such spiritual places and so romantic. I want to take Forrest and the kids this time. You must love it there."

"It was a wonderful place to grow up. Come by again anytime. You know, I was just thinking about the man you met that day, the one who was searching for answers about his mother. Remember, he told us she lived in Emerald Ridge and loved wines. We didn't recognize his name or his mother's. His name is Oliver Webb."

Madeline's eyes widened. "Wait a minute! I didn't put it together when I met him at the vineyards, but he's a guy around thirty looking for info on his mother who used to live in Emerald Ridge. He didn't give any real information, but could Oliver Webb be Lianna Dunhill and Archibald Fortune's son?"

"Well, the time frame matches," Penn interjected. "That's the same age."

"I mean, it's a long shot but a decent lead," Madeline said. "Thank you, Gia."

"I'm glad I could help," she said.

"You always help." Penn gave her a sideways wink. "I'll send a text to Hayes."

He had a group thread going with all the other siblings, including Hayes, and fired off a text.

Check into the name Oliver Webb. There might be a connection there. It's a promising lead.

Hayes responded right away: I'll get the PI on it.

"I've got to get back to work," Gia said. "Nice seeing you."

"Friday," Penn whispered as she brushed by him. "Don't forget."

"I won't," she said and squeezed his arm.

He stared at her backside as she walked out the door, her hips swaying just enough to drive him wild. He enjoyed every second. "Hey, Madeline," he said. "How good are you at keeping secrets?"

"I *hate* secrets." She frowned. "That's how we got into this mess."

She wasn't wrong.

"But this is a good secret."

"Okay, I'm listening."

"What do you know about diamond rings?" he asked.

She cocked her head, puzzled, holding up her ring finger. "I know where Forrest got mine and that's pretty much it. What's this about?"

"*That's* the secret."

He and Gia had agreed not to tell anyone in the family about their wedding, but from his perspective, Madeline was one of his sisters and he could use the help. She'd probably like to be involved and help her new brother in an area where he was clueless.

Besides, he'd swear her to secrecy and he'd bet his life he could count on her.

Chapter Ten

When Gia got back to the office after running into Penn and Madeline at the coffee shop, Leo and Antonia were waiting for her. Having heard the news from Bella, they congratulated Gia on getting the wine contract for all of Penn Fortune's hotels. She brushed it all off as "no big deal" but they didn't fall for it. It was a huge accomplishment for Leonetti wines, and that evening, they all went out to dinner at Lone Star Selects. Leo and his wife, Poppy Fortune, Antonia and Roth Fortune and Bella all joined in. Papa Enzo, her grandfather, didn't usually have to be talked into any celebration, so of course he was there, too. Even Mama came along, kissing and calling Gia *piccolo mio*—Italian for "my little one." To Mama, she'd always be the baby.

But if Antonia and Leo thought something different was going on with Gia, they gave no indication. Bella, earlier in the day, had kept giving her weird looks that seemed to ask, "Are you *okay*?" She supposed it wasn't normal to walk around with a goofy smile. But she had a secret. A delightful one. She was secretly, accidentally married to an amazing man and he wanted to *stay* married. She still couldn't believe it. If only he'd fall in love.

Gia had always wanted to fall for someone like Penn—a confident man with his own money who wanted to have a family with her. She wanted children, too, but she also wanted what her parents had had. A marriage based on true love. If Penn couldn't get there, there's no way this would ever work. She would not settle for his clinical idea of marriage.

Now, it was Friday night and she was going on a date with Penn. Her *husband.* She'd called him to ask him out when Adele gave her the idea. Her best friend said, right after telling her she shouldn't let him go, that she could *get* Penn to fall in love with her. Adele knew Gia could never stay married to someone who didn't love her. But as Adele mentioned, they'd basically just started *dating* and most people didn't fall in love that fast. Penn, since he sounded a bit jaded by his father's deception, would resist more than most. But that didn't mean it couldn't happen. She hoped her bestie was right as usual.

Gia tried on every date-night dress she owned and then wondered if she should ask Antonia to borrow *her* cute little black dress. It had pockets and Gia's little black dress did not. In the end, she decided to go for her own dress, lack of pockets notwithstanding. She paired it with her new pair of red Louboutin shoes. With any luck, he'd take one look at her and fall in love.

Either way, she had to risk this, because Adele was right: So much about Penn seemed perfect even if she was still getting to know him. He could wind up being just like every other guy she'd ever dated, minus the interest in her money.

Earlier today, Penn had said he'd send a car for her because he was wrapping up a meeting with a team overseas. She'd asked him where he had a local office and it turned out he didn't have one yet and simply worked out of the hotel's penthouse, occasionally grabbing a conference room downstairs if needed.

She arrived at the ritzy Emerald Ridge Hotel and pressed the button for his floor with a sense of déjà vu. They probably couldn't get into any more trouble than they already had, but just to be on the safe side, she wouldn't drink tonight. Not a sip.

She had not expected Penn to be waiting for her on the other side of the elevator when the doors rolled open. But there he was, and he looked...*drop-dead gorgeous*. He wore a dark suit, with a tie that matched the color of his mesmerizing green eyes. They crinkled when he smiled.

He did a slow slide up her body and held out his hand. "I hope you don't mind if we stay in tonight. It's just... I wanted to do something for you and I think you might think it's best not to do this in public."

Her mind went to all sorts of randy places and she quirked a brow. "Sounds intriguing. Whatever do you have in mind?"

"Get your mind out of the gutter, sweetheart," he chuckled, taking her hand and leading her into his suite. "I had dinner catered from Cucina. Because I wasn't sure what you liked, I ordered everything."

A white-clothed table for two was set up on the outdoor patio deck that overlooked the city lights below. Not only were there no takeout containers anywhere in view, but two tapered candles flickered in the center of a flower centerpiece. A chilled bottle of champagne sat next to the place settings and silverware.

"This is far more private than any restaurant. I love it."

"I wasn't sure how you felt about being seen in public yet," Penn said, helping her into her chair. "We're not going to tell anyone we're married, but can we let them know we're dating?"

Gia hadn't considered this but it was a good point. Maybe while they figured out if they were going to stay married, they should also date in secret. This way if it didn't work out no one would ever have to know Penn had broken her heart. They might still be able to salvage a friendship out of this, more than she could say for any of her exes. Another branch of the Fortunes and Leonettis were already somewhat intertwined in marriage. For this one to blow up after they'd tried might be another scandal.

"Honestly, I hadn't considered it, but I think it *is* best to keep everything a secret. For now."

"I'll follow your lead, since you're the one putting the brakes on."

The words were said lightly but Gia heard the frustration behind them. Surely, though, he could understand her reluctance.

The risotto, lasagna and smoked salmon penne from the restaurant were delicious, especially when Penn kept stealing sexy glances at her over the candles. She decided to indulge in one glass of champagne. The view of the bustling city below, the handsome man across from her, and the champagne he poured were too perfect. But then Penn reached in his pocket and set a small black box on the table with a slow smile. It was unexpected, and her heart skipped a beat, her palms suddenly sweaty.

"What's that?" Gia whispered. "For me?"

"It's the reason I thought we should stay in," Penn said. "Otherwise, we'd draw too much attention when I give it to you."

Gia opened it slowly, afraid to hope. It was a diamond wedding band, one more beautiful than she could have ever imagined.

"Penn…you didn't."

"No matter what happens, we got married. You deserved a lot more than that cheap bauble we found in the gift shop. This is more like you, isn't it?"

The hope and anticipation in his eyes were almost too

much. He wanted her to like it and of course she did. It was classic and elegant and looked extremely expensive.

"I love it." But it was still in the box.

Penn reached over, took it out and slipped it on her bare ring finger. "There. You *don't* need to wear it in public. But I'd appreciate if you wear it when you're with me."

She liked the thought of wearing this ring when they were together, like a reminder that she was his wife.

"I will," she promised. "I might even wear it when I'm alone." Then, unable to help herself, she added softly, "Don't worry, I'll…um…give you the ring back if we annul."

His expression darkened, and she caught a flicker of raw emotion in his eyes. "No. It's yours, no matter what you decide."

"That's too generous."

Penn cleared his throat. "I have a confession to make, because I don't want this marriage to start with lies," he said. "I had help buying that ring. In my defense, I had no idea what I was doing. I've never picked out a diamond ring before."

"Well, the salesclerk did a *great* job." Gia admired it in the fading light of the sunset.

"Well, that's where my confession comes in." Penn winced. "I…had to tell someone about us."

"We said we weren't going to tell anyone," Gia said, cheeks flushing because she'd confided in Adele. "Who did you tell?"

"Madeline," Penn said.

"But she…she's part of your family. Won't she tell someone?"

"I swore her to secrecy, and honestly, she was excited to help me. She said she'd never had a brother and this was the kind of thing she'd always pictured doing."

"Oh, that's sweet. I'm glad you asked her, then." Gia cleared her throat. "I don't want to lie to you, either."

Penn cocked his head.

"Um, I…may have also told someone." Gia waved her hand dismissively. "But no one in my *family*, of course. They are the worst secret keepers in the world. I confided in my best friend, Adele—who works for me—that we got married. She won't tell anyone."

Penn laughed. "Guess it's kind of tough to keep a secret of this magnitude from everyone."

"If we manage for a week, I'll be very impressed with us." Gia admired her ring again. "What did Madeline think of what we'd done?"

"I held back the details, because I wanted to protect your privacy. Basically, she thinks I'm going to ask you to marry me and she needs to keep *that* a secret."

Gia had to admit he was ingeniously smart. "Does she approve?"

"Very much so. Does Adele approve of me?" He grinned, those eyes crinkling again.

"Yes, in fact, she suggested I ask you out on a date."

"I like her already." Penn brought Gia's hand to his lips and brushed a kiss across her knuckles.

"She made the point that I haven't really given this a chance." Gia stopped just short of mentioning her plan of getting him to fall in love with her. *Baby steps.*

"That's true." Penn rose from the table, took Gia's hand and pulled her up. "I appreciate you keeping your mind open to staying married."

"I admit it's hard to say no to you."

"Don't let me pressure you too much. Let me know if I make you uncomfortable. In business, I almost always get my way."

"I'm not surprised." But Gia refused to be another one of Penn Fortune's successful *business* deals.

"The key word is *almost.*" Penn poured from the already uncorked champagne bottle and offered her a flute. "A toast to staying married."

"To staying married." Gia took only a sip and put it down. "You never thought of asking someone to marry you before me?"

"I thought about it. Especially with one long-term relationship which lasted a couple of years, but in the end I never got there." He drank from his flute.

"Aw, did she break your heart?"

Penn's mouth flattened into a hard line, his gaze dropping for the briefest second. "No, I don't think I ever gave it to her."

So, he'd never fallen in love. This did *not* bode well. It could be Penn's heart was closed up long before he ever found out about his father's indiscretions.

He set his glass down. "What about you?"

"You already know about the guy who broke my heart. Marco was after my money and when we ended, he got cruel. Funny, he wanted to go ring shopping a few weeks before that but now I'm pretty sure he expected *me* to pay for the ring."

"Then we're both newbies." Penn closed the distance between them and pulled her into his arms. "I'm glad it's you."

"Because?" She was already addicted to this man, God help her.

"You understand me. You support me. We're alike in many ways."

She noticed he hadn't mentioned love but they'd established that was not important to him.

"I want to do all those things for you, too," Penn said. "Support you in every way."

He lowered his head to her mouth and kissed her deeply. Gia gripped the lapels of his button-up and was lost in him. He made it too easy to fall in love. She was already halfway there. *Slow down, Gia*. Don't get too far ahead or you'll crash and burn.

"God, Gia," Penn groaned. "You taste so good."

They had chemistry that went on for days and, even if she wanted more, this was how it always started. Intimacy began with carnal pleasure between two people who were attracted to each other and had a lot in common. Then sometimes it deepened into love and a truer kind of intimacy and trust. She had to give love time to grow. He'd get there…at least, she hoped.

He blew out the candles, took her hand and led her inside the apartment, shutting the French patio doors behind them.

Then she was in his arms again, trembling as his mouth slid down the column of her neck, kissing every bare inch of skin. His agile hands slid down the zipper on her dress, caressing her bare shoulders, reaching for her breasts. When her dress slipped to the ground, she stepped out of it. His gaze slowly slid up her body, taking in her red push-up bra and matching thongs.

"You're killing me," he growled, his teeth grazing against his lower lip.

"Then maybe you'll die happy." She curled her arms around his neck and pressed her body against his.

"No doubt." Then he picked her up in his arms and led her to his bed.

Chapter Eleven

Penn had his arms full of gorgeous Gia and didn't want to let go.

They'd had two rounds of incredible, balls-to-the-wall sex, which would always headline his greatest fantasies. Hopefully, he'd done his job to convince her how good they were together, how amazing this lifelong partnership between them could be. He'd gone for a personal best tonight, and given her response, he'd accomplished his goal.

"Stay the night."

"Hmm." Gia lay beside him with one leg thrown over his, her cheek pressed to his chest.

He would take that as a yes. Considering how passionate and reciprocating she'd been to him all night, he'd guess she wanted some sleep. He had no idea how *he'd* actually sleep all night with her in his arms. Probably much like he did the last time this happened, when he couldn't keep his eyes open anymore and exhaustion claimed him.

He tugged on a lock of her hair. "When can I see you again?"

"Sunday? But now it's my turn to plan a date," Gia mumbled.

"You're on. What are we doing?"

"Come to the Leonetti family vineyard and you'll find out."

"Uh-oh. Are you going to put me to work picking grapes?" he joked.

"That might be a good cover," she chuckled. "But no. I will have to make up some excuse as to why you're visiting the vineyards since we're not officially dating. My family will ask too many questions if I don't."

"You can tell them I've come to see how all the wines I bought for my hotels are produced and bottled."

"Exactly." She propped up on her chin and batted her eyelashes. "And then, when no one is looking, I'll pull you into the empty cask room and have my way with you."

At that, he had to laugh. "Good thing I don't have to be talked into anything when it comes to you. Sign me up."

"Last night was amazing." She brushed a kiss across his pec.

"Nothing less than I expected." He toyed with her hair, winding a lock around his finger. "We're a true partnership in every way."

He felt her tense in his arms and realized too late he'd said the wrong thing.

"We're not lovers?" she murmured, her voice barely above a whisper.

He had to tread carefully here. Technically, yes, *of course* they were. But she wanted to hear they were falling for each other. He didn't want to promise what he couldn't give her. It would be cruel to lead her on. Sex could stay uncomplicated when love wasn't in the picture. That was the way it should be. No messy entanglements. No cheating and tears. It made all the sense in the world. If not, why were so many arranged marriages successful?

When he didn't respond, she sat up in bed, bringing the sheets up to cover her breasts. Not a good sign.

"What does a true partnership mean to you in a marriage?

Are you going to stay faithful to me even if you're not in love?"

A muscle ticked in his jaw. "I told you I would be faithful to you. Always."

"But the main reason couples stay faithful to each other is being in love. When no one else will do, you won't consider cheating. It's hard to believe you'll always be faithful when falling in love can make people a little nuts. If not me, you might one day fall for someone else, outside of our marriage. Then what?"

"Well, as you know, that happens all the time in so-called love connections. Losing your heart to one person, then the next. I won't do that, but you've just made my point—falling in love makes people crazy. That won't happen to us because I won't *let* it."

Her gaze softened. "Oh, Penn. Sometimes mad and messy can be amazing. I feel sorry for you if you've never felt that way about someone."

He had no words, but relief poured through him when she lay back down in his arms and snuggled. With one hand, Penn reached for the remote to turn off the lights and roll the window shades down.

"Let's go to sleep, sweetheart." He tugged her close in the circle of his arms and held on tight because he didn't want her going anywhere.

The next morning after Gia left, Penn checked his emails and tried to catch up on work he'd let slide on Friday. The date with Gia couldn't have gone any better and he looked forward to more time with her tomorrow. The ring had been a success, and he had Madeline to thank. Dinner and ambience were stellar, sex off the charts, conversation stimulating. This was all headed in a good direction and Penn could sense he'd get his way. After all, he did not look forward to getting an annulment and having to watch Gia date some other loser like Marco. No, she belonged to him. He could make her happy and he'd keep working until he convinced her they were a great team. She had some hang-ups about romantic love, and he'd simply have to convince her of his logic.

By lunchtime, he'd forgotten to eat, so he went to warm up some of last night's leftovers. But they weren't on the patio table where they'd left them. A mystery, as his housekeeper only came in once a week and never on a weekend. It couldn't be, but…yes, he found all the food put away in containers and there was only one explanation. *Gia.* She'd probably done this before she left, when he was still in the shower.

He warmed up a plate of smoked salmon penne and fired off an email to her:

Thanks for putting the food away. You didn't have to do that.

Gia replied: Thank goodness we covered it or the birds might have had a feast. Enjoy your leftovers! Dinner was delicious.

He was halfway through his plate when his phone buzzed again. This time, a text from Hayes in the siblings group:

The PI found Oliver Webb! He's a wealthy rancher in Austin. He IS our missing brother (having the name made this much easier!)

So, Penn had yet another brother. That made three brothers and three sisters that Archibald Fortune had sired. Busy man, his father. Obviously he considered his seed so special it had to be spread far and wide.

A text from Madeline popped up: Finally! This is wonderful. Thanks for hiring the PI and all your hard work on this.

Hayes replied: Don't get too excited. The DNA test will have to confirm, but his mother had an affair with Archibald and he didn't know who his father was until she died. The timing fits. But Oliver isn't sure he wants anything to do with us. Obviously, he has his own money and doesn't need his share of the inheritance. Remind you of anyone, Penn?

Penn snorted and didn't reply. It was true he hadn't wanted anything to do with the mess created out of Archibald's deceit, but then his mother had begged him to get involved. No one would get a dime if they didn't find the youngest sibling, and everything would be tied up forever. And once Hayes's paternity was established, Penn had no reason not to help his brother to his share of the Fortune wealth.

Shelby, ever the optimist, wrote: At least we found him. That was our main responsibility. Maybe now the will can be executed.

There was a flurry of texts from the other sisters, all with various opinions on when and how this might happen, and why Oliver might not want to be involved with any of this. Penn found it obvious that Oliver would need time to process. It made sense he'd be unsure how he felt about being the abandoned son of a billionaire. Chances were, he could have used his father's support at one time.

Jillian texted: Hopefully he will accept the land in Emerald Ridge our father left him. It's the only way we can uncover the secrets of what might be buried there.

You're not the only one who wants to find out. It could explain our father's past and we might find closure with his deception and betrayal, Hayes replied.

Penn hoped so, but nothing would excuse Archibald's behavior.

Just then, he received a ring from the penthouse elevator to his suite. The camera showed his mother, Damaris, whom he hadn't been expecting. She lived in the building, too, and lately, she'd been very needy, focusing most of her attention on Penn since Hayes was now married with a child.

Hayes opened the door to let her inside.

His mother reached to give him a quick hug. "I don't want to intrude but just checking in."

"You're always welcome." He led her into the kitchen and offered her some iced tea from the pitcher he always had in there.

Damaris Fortune was still beautiful in her late fifties, still carried herself with sophistication and a quiet nature some people interpreted as aloof. But no one had ever loved a man the way his mother loved Archibald Fortune. Penn saw first-hand the love between his parents on a daily basis but had never zeroed in on the fact his mother loved far more intently than his father ever had. When he didn't show up for holiday celebrations, she always made some lame excuse for him. Only after his death would they find out he was juggling families, so no wonder he couldn't see Damaris on every holiday. When he died suddenly from a heart attack, she'd been shattered. Afterwards, as if to dice after cutting, came the news of all his other wives.

His other families.

Penn had never hated his father so much as in the moment he saw the agony in his mother's eyes. She'd been forced to meet these other women and their children at the reading of the will. His mother had never signed up for this humiliation.

Because she was here, he gave her the news from the PI about Oliver Webb, so she'd know how close they were to finalizing the inheritance.

She brightened and clapped her hands. “That’s wonderful! Oh, Penn, now you can finally think about settling down.”

He almost choked on his tea. “Um, what does that have to do with anything?”

“Hayes is married with a little family, which, granted, came as a surprise, but now it’s your turn.”

Penn laughed and shook his head, finding the irony almost too much. “That’s not how it works.”

“If Hayes can do it, you can, too.” She took a sip of her tea and set it down. “I can’t have Archibald’s deceit ruining my son’s future happiness. You don’t have to wind up like him, you know.”

“He isn’t going to ruin me, but I can’t stand what he did to you. I’ll never forgive him for that.”

“While I appreciate your loyalty, I don’t want you hanging on to that kind of hate. I’ve come to a peace about this. Archibald didn’t only betray me, but all of us. Now I have a little community of people surrounding me who understand what I’ve been through. Except for maybe Taffy, most of us wives all support each other because we’re going through the same thing. And we’re working on Taffy.”

Penn figured this was as good a time as any to lay the groundwork. “Actually, I’m thinking about settling down. You’re right, I want children and a family. I’m determined to do much better than my father did.”

“That’s great, Penn.” Her smile was wider than he’d seen in a while. “Is it anyone I know?”

“It’s too soon to tell. I’m not sure this woman…well, I’m not all that sure she realizes how good we could be together.”

“What?” She blinked. “She must be insane.”

Penn snorted. “Please.”

“You’re a catch. You have it all. Looks, personality, intelligence. Money. The important thing is to find a woman who isn't fixated on all your money. You'll have even more now. For that reason, be careful." She tapped her chin thoughtfully. "Actually, a good woman for you might be someone who already has her own money."

Penn couldn't have said it better himself.

"Good point. I'll see whether I can find someone like that."

Chapter Twelve

Gia spent most of Saturday and part of Sunday preparing for her date with Penn.

She'd told him to show up in the afternoon and she'd give him the full tour. More than anything, she wanted to share with him her love for this land, which had meant so much to her growing up in a close-knit Italian family.

She drove down the long dirt lane that led to the villa where it had all started over a hundred years ago. The grounds were lush and green, filled with rows upon rows of vines. The family's Tuscan-style mansion was separated from the villa by a clearing. The Leonetti's large, extended family lived in the mansion, each family unit with their separate wing.

The only reason she'd moved out of the home where her family still resided was because Marco had talked her into it when they moved in together. He'd had his eye on a swanky condo in downtown Emerald Ridge with all amenities. Of course, she'd had to pay for most of it. The thing was, Gia didn't mind spotty Wi-Fi reception outside of town, or the fact the old, classic buildings had zero "smart house" upgrades. Out here she was reminded of her roots. It had all started with a patch of fertile land that her great-grandparents had lived and breathed. With it, they'd started a family business and a legacy.

Someday she would like to move back, maybe with her

husband to raise their family. They could live in a separate wing of the main house, but her children would be able to see their grandma and great-grandpa daily. They'd run in the same fields that generations of Leonettis had, but they might be Fortunes, too.

Okay, stop getting carried away. Her dream of a family and a husband wasn't as close as one would think given her marital status. Penn *acted* like a man in love, but as the consummate businessman, he let logic drive him. He'd simply given her the ring because he wanted to impress her with what he could buy, the life he could give her if she stayed with him. She didn't want any of those things, just him. His heart. Now she had a new plan. She wouldn't talk about love anymore, but just let it happen. If he could fall in love with her, she'd stay married to him.

But if he couldn't? Well, then she'd just have to hope she could walk away with her heart intact.

As she pulled her sedan up to the main house, she saw Papa Enzo seated in a rocking chair on the wraparound front porch, a blanket thrown over him. Gia slipped off her wedding ring, put it back in the box and stuffed it in her bag. She'd had to take it off yesterday when she went to book club with Mama, Bella and Antonia, but she hadn't been lying when she told Penn she'd wear it when she was alone, too. She had, all day, lifting it up to the light in appreciation but mostly imagining spending a life with the man who chose it.

She parked and walked up to Papa Enzo, waving to him as she closed the distance. The scent of grapes lay thick and heavy in the June air.

"Ah, piccolo mio! Come stai?" Papa Enzo said, holding his arms wide.

She went right into his embrace. "I'm fine but how are you?"

Last year, her grandfather had had a brush with cancer. But luckily it was now in remission and he was spryer than many other men in their early eighties. Still, Gia worried about him all the time.

"Buono." Papa patted her hand. "It is good to see you."

"I wanted to let you know, Penn Fortune asked for a tour today."

Papa shook a finger. "Smart man. Always check out what you bought. Make sure it's first-rate."

"I thought I'd get here early and prep a little."

"It is Sunday, so no work today." He chuckled and shook his head. "Even Bella is home with the children."

Papa always gave his vineyard staff Sundays off to be with their families. It was the reason he had low turnover rate and ranch hands who'd been with the family for more than forty years.

"That's okay, I planned to do it myself. I know where everything is."

She would take the picnic basket they used for some of the tastings and do a nice spread for Penn. Cheeses, sliced salami, olives and crackers.

"Papa." Gia hesitated a moment but if anyone had the answer to this, it would be Enzo. "Do you think two people who get married should first be compatible or is it more important to be in love?"

His eyes brightened. "You are thinking of a special man?"

"No," she lied. "It's just the other day I was watching one of those reality TV shows where couples get engaged without ever seeing each other."

"What kind of show is this?" He blinked.

Gia shook her head and laughed. "You wouldn't be interested. Oh, it's silly, but it made me think of days in the old country. You know, when some marriages were arranged by the families."

"I wouldn't know. The first moment I laid eyes on your grandmother, it was like Cupid himself struck me with an arrow." He patted his chest. "Love like that doesn't come along often."

Exactly what Gia wanted—a man struck with love and overwhelmed by the depth of his feelings for her. She'd never imagined settling for anything else, and now here she was actually considering it because the man was Penn. Because did she really want to get an annulment and watch him marry someone else? If he truly fell in love, she'd want that for him, even if she couldn't stand by and watch it happen.

"That's what I thought," she murmured wistfully. "I want a love like that."

Papa nodded. "Now, my grandparents, *that* was an arranged marriage."

"Are you kidding me?"

Gia had to have heard wrong. Papa Enzo's grandparents had started the vineyard in 1903, and there were photos of them everywhere. They'd had a large family and those who remembered them said they were always together, in an almost ridiculous way. Like both sides of a coin, or two best friends. You couldn't find a single family picture in which they weren't side by side. Family legend said they never spent a single night apart after marriage.

Papa laughed and shrugged. "I know, it's silly to young people today, but it was the way her family did things in Italy. For all four of their daughters, they scouted for the right men. It was important they be well matched in every way. More important than love, I suppose."

"But...they sounded so in love. Mama said they were ridiculous, always having to be together, kissing and holding hands like a couple of teenagers."

He shrugged. "Love grew. My grandmother was very beautiful, you see. Looked like Sophia Loren when she was young. I suppose my father couldn't resist falling in love, seeing everything else was right, too."

Seeing everything else was right, too.

"But, what if they'd never fallen in love?"

"They would have lived happily anyway because they were well matched. Some of us are lucky, others have our parents intervene. I'm sure not all arranged marriages were as successful. But, amore mio, marriage is more complicated than simply being in love. That's just the fun part."

Gia smirked. "Things are different today. Most people don't need to get married for the fun part."

"I'm an old man but I know these things. The thing to remember is, in a long marriage, you're going to have times when you don't think about your beloved day and night like you did when you first fell in love. Children, for instance, come along and insist on some attention." He chuckled and shook his head. "But that doesn't mean the love is gone. It just grows stronger and sturdier until it's hard to knock down in a strong wind. Like a good vine."

"I knew you were somehow going to bring it back to the grapes." Gia laughed and tucked the blanket around him.

"It's your legacy." He patted her hand. "And don't you forget it."

Chapter Thirteen

The wide skies over the plains of Texas were tinged with blue from one end of the horizon to the other. Penn drove out to the Leonetti Vineyards that his sister Madeline had raved about. Being new to Emerald Ridge, he'd never been here. Today was a perfect day, the late spring day warm without a cloud in the sky.

At the entrance, a large, weathered wooden sign in classic lettering, read Leonetti Vineyards, Established 1903. Then he spied perfection if the word itself were to take shape. Gia stood at the entrance to the Tuscan-style villa, her long, dark hair loose and blowing in the slight breeze. She wore a white dress that hit just above her knees and Western-style boots with blue tooling. But she could wear anything, or *nothing at all*, and still be the most beautiful woman he'd ever seen.

He rolled the window down. "Hello, miss. I'm lost. Is this where I can find the yellow brick road?"

She threw back her head and laughed. "No, but something better. Just pull over there and I'll give you a tour."

The tour was a small part of why he'd come here. Penn had been to vineyards in Italy and France and seen the best of the best. He was here to get to know his wife better, to see if he could find any reason *he* should be the one to annul this marriage. But other than the fact she seemed determined there should be romantic love in a marriage, he saw no reason *not* to stay married. Gia was an intelligent woman, and in the end he didn't see her turning down the opportunity to merge their considerable assets. They made a great team, and sooner or later she'd see it, too.

Had it been anybody else, Penn would have probably rushed the paperwork for the annulment through. But this was *Gia Leonetti.* He'd be an idiot not to want this to work. She was gorgeous, kind, intelligent and loyal. It would be a damn shame not to pass on those genes, but he didn't care if she couldn't have children. At one time, he might have seen that as a problem. But she'd made him realize the measure and worth of a woman was far more than whether she could have biological children.

She met him halfway and stuck out her hand to shake. "Welcome to Leonetti Vineyards. Play along."

A few feet away behind her, he spied an older gentleman, who'd appeared out of nowhere.

He waved. "Buongiorno!"

Gia turned and he followed her lead. "Papa, this is Penn Fortune. Penn, meet my grandfather, Enzo Leonetti."

Penn closed the distance between them and shook the family patriarch's hand. "Hello, sir."

"I know some of your family. The Fortunes and Leonettis have merged bloodlines."

Penn quirked a brow, wondering if Gia had told him about their marriage, but she quietly shook her head. "My sister Antonia and brother Leo are both married to Fortunes."

"Oh, yes. My distant cousins. That's another branch of the family." Penn shook his head. "Apparently, there are a lot of us. In fact, far more than even I realized."

If Enzo caught his meaning, he was too kind to laugh. By now, everyone in town knew Archibald Fortune had somehow managed to have three wives and five children at the same time. Some joked it was no wonder he had a heart attack.

"Family. It is always a blessing," Enzo said. "Well, I am going back to my rocking chair now. I just wanted to greet you."

"Your villa is beautiful. It reminds me of Tuscany."

"You've been? That's exactly what my relatives intended. They arrived from Tuscany, intent on building a family legacy here. Please enjoy. My lovely granddaughter will give you the tour." Enzo waved and shuffled back across a clearing.

Gia pointed. "That's the family home in the back. I found him on the front porch, enjoying the day, so I told him you were arriving for a tour."

No sooner was Enzo out of sight than Penn pulled Gia into his arms. "Damn, I've missed you."

He gave her a long and lingering kiss, until she came up for air, smiling, and pushed against his chest.

"Missed you, too," she said breathlessly. "But let's save that business for later."

"All right. Show me where the magic happens."

She tugged on his hand and led him in the direction of the vineyards. He followed her through rows upon rows of grapes, into the bottling and dark casking rooms, stealing another kiss along the way. They went into the tasting room where another flight sat on the granite bar beside a tray filled with cheeses and crackers. It threw him back to the night they were married.

"Dangerous. Are we doing this again?"

"Well, we certainly can't get any more *married* than we already are," she said, pouring from a bottle of dark red wine. "But no, we're not drinking too much this time."

"After all, I need to drive back." He took a bite of cheese.

"This is where you used to live? Damn, rough life. Tell me, how did you survive it all?"

She smirked and stuck out her tongue. "I know how lucky I am, believe me. And in case I want to forget, Papa Enzo reminds me all the time."

"He seems like a good man."

"Last year, he had a cancer scare but he's doing well now. Sometimes I do think about moving back to the big house, just so I can keep an eye on him. But it's not like my mother doesn't do a great job of that."

"Why did you move out? Privacy?" He imagined it would be tough to get some peace and quiet with family everywhere you looked.

She frowned. "I was talked into moving into one of those luxury condos in town."

"Like my place?"

"Not quite as fancy," she told him.

"Who talked you into it?"

"He's not worth discussing." She handed him a glass. "The privacy is nice, I admit, but the truth is I've always pictured raising my kids here. This is where Bella lives with her children. Same with Leo and Antonia."

"Cousins are built-in playmates."

"True, but the point is, I've always wanted to raise my own family here on the farm. I'm a farm girl at heart. I know that's not my gift—it's talking to people and making deals. Bella has a gift for grapes and knowing when they've reached perfect maturity. But I can make our deals because I believe so much in our product and what we do here."

"It shows, sweetheart." He reached for her hand and squeezed it.

"What do you think about raising children here? Would you do it?"

The open vulnerability in her tone made his chest pinch. He grinned. "Would I be able to live here with them?"

She cocked her head and gave him a "are you for real" look. "Why, yes, if you're the father."

He touched his heart as if he'd been speared. "Yes, I'd love to have my children, which God willing would also be *your* children, raised here. By now maybe you realize I'll be a different kind of father than the one I had."

"I know you will be, but are you sure about raising the children here? Even without Wi-Fi and shades that roll up with the press of a remote?"

"Are you making fun of my penthouse?" he said. "I lived my entire life having to roll up my own window shades, I'll have you know."

She laughed. "You're cute, Penn."

"*Cute?* That's what you think of me?" He pretended to be wounded by the offhand compliment.

"Don't fish for praise. Fine, you're devastatingly handsome."

"That's better. No matter where we live, I'll be available to my children. I won't miss sports games because of work; that's where delegating comes in."

"I'm glad to hear it and I will be the same way."

They finished the flight and he pulled her into his arms again, pressing a kiss against her temple. "This is a good day."

She wrapped her arms around his neck and smiled up at him. "It doesn't have to be over."

"I don't want it to be." He kissed her again, on the lips this time. "You know, I didn't want to come to Emerald Ridge. I was happy living in Houston but my mother and brother needed me here. But you've been the best part of this town and you're not anything I ever expected."

"My papa would say that's the sweetest part of life…the unexpected."

Gia took his hand and tugged him out of the dark casking room back outside into the sunshine. They walked up a small hill to the top and a row of grapes labeled Chardonnay.

"I used to run in these fields with my brother and sisters," Gia confessed. "But this was my favorite row. From here you can see everything."

She was right. The angle was perfect for a view of the surrounding lower hills, the lush green valley, and the house below.

"Once, I actually hung a blanket between the two rows and tried to make a fort."

"You what?" He pictured young and adventurous Gia, who loved to sleep outside under the stars. "What were you picturing inside your fort?"

"Oh, that I was a princess who ruled over a small country."

He chuckled, impressed she wanted an entire country and not just a palace.

"I got in trouble for it." She chewed on her lower lip. "My father was pretty strict about the grapes. This is our product. I heard a lot about how it's not a game but our livelihood. So I never did it again."

Penn drew her into his arms. "Thanks for sharing that with me. So, what you're telling me is if we have a little girl, I had better look out. She might be as imaginative as her mother."

"With a father who flies planes. Between the two of us, I think our future children might actually be in trouble."

"It won't be boring, that's for sure."

Penn kissed her, picturing an entire life laid out before him, and for the first time in his life, none of it scared him.

Chapter Fourteen

When Penn arrived to work on Monday, he had a little spring in his step, probably because he'd spent most of the weekend with Gia, winding up in bed each night. They were a good fit, and what's more, it seemed Gia might finally believe so, too. She hadn't mentioned anything more about falling in love or silly romantic aspirations. They'd talked more about kids, how they'd raise them, schools and family vacations. She was smart enough to see what they had was real. Solid. All they truly needed.

He could practically see their children running around the vineyards, soaking up all their Italian heritage. Hopefully, she'd be open to having three or four kids, but any children they raised together would be a true blessing. Penn definitely saw himself as a hands-on father, completely the opposite of his own absentee one. His kids would never have to wonder if he'd show up for Thanksgiving or Christmas or any other special occasion. He'd *always* be there.

His morning went by quickly as he had Zoom meetings on expansion and planning with staff in Italy, where he would bring a Fortune Resort Hotel in the next five years. Penn sometimes dressed his top half for these meetings in a shirt and tie, and wore jeans no one could see. But sooner or later, if he was staying in Emerald City like his family wanted, he should find office space.

He sifted through the mail, finding nothing interesting until he got to a letter postmarked Las Vegas, Nevada. The marriage certificate had arrived. He should have it framed but best not to get ahead of himself. Just because he was proud of being married to Gia, didn't mean she was proud to be married to him. Something told him she wasn't going to settle, but he kept ignoring that niggling voice. Just like in business, he worked hard, expected the best outcome, and usually got it.

Things between them were going so well he didn't expect she'd consider annulling now, but it would be disingenuous not to tell her the truth. The plan was to wait to consider annulling at least until the certificate arrived. He picked up the phone to text her, then reconsidered. Maybe he'd just present it to her tonight at dinner along with the suggestion they leave things as they were. She'd asked him to cook for her and he'd promised he'd try, but he'd probably just order in.

Penn's phone buzzed with a text from Hayes:

Hey, me and Flora are at Emerald Park with Mateo. Drop by on your lunch hour if you get a break. You haven't seen much of your nephew.

Since the time Penn had arrived in Emerald Ridge, he'd had little time to hang out with Hayes's family. Instead, he'd been locked in terrible meetings that too often involved Madeline's mother, Taffy Fortune, a woman Penn couldn't stand. But he missed hanging out with his brother. Seeing him fall into his role as a new father to his adorable baby boy was both inspiring and a little jarring. Penn responded:

I'll be there in a few.

He could easily walk to Emerald Park, which was in the middle of downtown near his hotel. There were plenty of kids out on this summer day with school out and he had to search through the groups to find Hayes with his family. This year, his little brother had discovered that the casual relationship he'd had with Flora had resulted in a child he hadn't known about. Just like that, Hayes had himself a ready-made family, and Penn couldn't be happier for him.

"Hey!" Hayes waved Penn over. "Come over and say hi."

Penn walked toward Hayes and the artificial pond where Mateo was holding Flora's hand and watching the ducks. As usual, his rodeo cowboy brother wore a black Stetson that Penn had to admit was an advantage in the midday heat.

A little self-conscious about his outfit, Penn loosened his tie and rolled up the sleeves of his button-up. "Only my bottom half is dressed for the park."

"That's okay." Hayes elbowed Penn. "It 'suits' you. Ha, get it?"

Penn smirked. "I see you're already telling dad jokes."

"Being a father is the best thing ever." Hayes beamed in the direction of his fiancée, Flora, and their son.

"When did he start walking?" Penn asked.

"Two weeks ago, he started toddling around and shocked us both. Flora says he's young to start walking."

Flora joined them, holding Mateo against her hip. "Hey, Uncle Penn."

He gave her a quick sideways embrace. "I'm sorry I haven't been around much, but that's going to change."

"Yeah? Are you considering a permanent move to Emerald Ridge?" Hayes slung an arm around Flora, bringing them both closer to him. "It would be nice if we could raise our children in the same town."

"That *could* happen. Let's just say I may have met someone," Penn said. "And it's potentially serious."

Hayes and Flora exchanged a look and Hayes whistled. "Hoo boy! I never thought I'd see *you* settle down."

"That could have been said about both of us," Penn retorted. "And now look at you."

Hayes smiled at Flora, the look of utter tenderness and love so glaringly obvious that anyone could see it. Even with their checkered family history, Hayes was bravely attempting to make his relationship work. Penn didn't blame him, because being with the mother of his child was the right thing to do. What he *didn't* understand was why Hayes had felt it necessary to fall in love. It seemed he was risking too much.

There was so much involved in keeping a family together that adding in a deep romantic love into the mix seemed impractical and unnecessary when a marriage with children needed a solid foundation. When he thought of his own parents, he pictured all the passion between them, with the end result of each of them having affairs with other people.

"Well, how about a little trial by fire?" Flora said, setting her boy down. "Mateo wants to feed the ducks."

"Yeah, *Uncle Penn*," Hayes said, pulling out and handing him a bag of feed. "Jump right in."

"Okay," Penn said, not easily scared. "Let's go, little buddy."

Mateo wasn't shy and held up his little hand, which Penn nearly swallowed in his own.

"Duck," Mateo said. "Duck-duck."

"He's already *talking*?" Penn turned to Hayes. "This kid is a genius."

"Believe it or not, that's his first word." Hayes rolled his eyes. "I had hoped for dada. No, we get *duck*."

"Duck-duck," Mateo said, toddling along with Penn toward the lake, holding his hand.

Penn had the most enjoyable time of his day helping Mateo

feed the ducks, watching the utter delight that took over his face whenever he threw the feed into the lake. With kids, simple things brought joy. Penn couldn't wait to have a child of his own. When they ran out of food, they walked back to Hayes and Flora, who were sitting on a bench not so discreetly making out.

Penn cleared his throat and they came up for air.

"All done?" Hayes said, reaching for his son.

"Duck!" Mateo threw back his head and laughed with delight.

"He *really* loves ducks," Penn said. "Should I buy him one for his birthday?"

Hayes quirked a brow. "A duck?"

"Duck!" Mateo said and clapped his hands.

"I could have a duck pond installed for him. You forget, I have contacts through my hotels." Penn wanted to dote on his nephew and he didn't see the issue.

"Maybe just a stuffed one for now?" Flora smiled.

"Ah, I get it." Penn tipped back on his heels. "I'm getting carried away."

"It's not just you," Hayes said, quirking a brow. "Mom suggested buying him his own *pony*."

"Sounds like we need an intervention," Penn laughed, turning and doing a double take when he saw Gia walking alone down the sidewalk that ran past the park. "Wait here a sec. I'll be right back."

He rushed to catch up with her before she walked past them. She was dressed for work in a pantsuit, her hair up in a bun.

He stepped in front of her. "Hey, there."

She smiled. "What are *you* doing here?"

"I was at the park when I saw you walking by." He took

her hand and pulled her along. "There's someone I want you to meet."

He brought her over and introduced her to Hayes, Flora and Mateo. Gia was as gracious as Penn would have expected.

"I've heard so much about you, Hayes. It's nice to meet you, Flora." She patted Mateo's back. "Hello, cutie."

"Duck." Mateo smiled shyly and buried his face in his mother's neck.

"That's all he can say right now," Penn said. "But we're hopeful."

"You're Antonia and Leo's sister, right?" Hayes asked.

Gia nodded. "Yes, that's right."

"And…how do you two know each other?" Hayes gestured between her and Penn.

Penn exchanged a glance with Gia, hoping she'd pipe in, but when she hesitated, he answered. "Actually, we're in business together. She just secured a deal with me to supply my hotels with Leonetti wines."

"Congratulations," Hayes said, his arm securely around Flora like they were surgically attached.

"Thank you," Gia replied. "It was nice seeing you, but I need to get to my next meeting."

"I'll walk you back," Penn offered.

He still had to tell her about the marriage certificate. They reached the end of the pathway and entrance to the park.

"I was going to text you—the marriage certificate arrived." He took a deep breath and went for it. "And it's almost been a week. I'm hoping you'll decide to stay married. You've just seen firsthand what we could have. Mateo is adorable. Don't you want that?"

"Of course," she said, not meeting his eyes. "You know I want a family."

"Then let's do it, Gia." He took both of her hands in his.

"We don't need all the trappings of romantic love. All those ups and downs in love make life disruptive for children."

"Really? You believe that? He seems pretty happy and well-adjusted to me."

She looked past him in the direction of Hayes and Flora, and okay, he took her point.

"We don't know they will last. I hope so, but there are no guarantees simply because they're in love right now and everything is perfect. What we have is *better.* A true partnership because we both want the same things and we don't have the messiness of love complicating our lives."

"I don't know," Gia said, biting her lower lip. "I need more time."

"Okay," he said, lowering his head. "Take all the time you need."

"See you tonight," she said, walking away quickly.

He watched her leave but she hadn't gone far before a man stopped her. Penn didn't recognize him, but he acted far too familiar with Gia for his taste. They started walking together. That was his *wife* the man was clearly flirting with. A strange emotion filled Penn, one he barely recognized. *Jealousy.* What the hell was wrong with him? This was one of the problems with romantic love. That overwhelming feeling of wanting to possess someone completely. No, it wasn't right. He wouldn't have it. All that untampered emotion wasn't healthy.

Hayes came up to him. "Okay, that's *her*, isn't it? The one you might be getting serious with."

"Yeah, I don't know anymore."

Penn had a terrible feeling this business deal was not going to end the way he'd like.

Chapter Fifteen

By the time Gia returned from her errand to buy fresh baked cookies from the bakery for her and Adele, she'd lost her appetite.

"What's wrong?" Adele stood. "They didn't have salted caramel cookies?"

Gia dropped the box on Adele's desk and went past her into the office without a word. At the park, she'd witnessed exactly what she wanted. What she'd longed for all her life. A love like that of her parents and grandparents. She'd seen it today in Hayes and Flora. They were blessed with an adorable little boy but the love between them extended far beyond the child they'd created. It practically emanated through their skin with a shimmering glow.

Then as she left Penn, she'd run into an old friend, Michael, who'd wasted no time in asking her out point-blank. She'd made some lame excuse because she couldn't tell him she was *married* and therefore dating him wouldn't be appropriate. But honestly, she wasn't at all sure she'd stay married, so she should consider giving him a call. Michael was no Penn Fortune, but he was a handsome and successful guy who owned a gym.

"Okay, what's up?" Adele shut the door to the inner office and took a seat.

Gia buried her face in her hands. "Oh, nothing."

Her best friend twitched her finger. "You better talk, girlfriend, because they *did* have your salted caramel cookies and I bet you didn't even eat a single one on the way back. You must be sick or something."

"Heartsick."

"Why?"

"This isn't working. Penn doesn't *love* me. We spent hours in bed this weekend, I took him to the vineyard and he met my grandfather. Penn told me he'd love to raise our children at the vineyard."

"See? That's great!" Adele said. "Progress."

"Today, he let me know the certificate came but we should stay married even if we're not in love because love is so chaotic and unpredictable."

"Oh." Adele's face smile dropped.

"He said this right after I met his brother Hayes and Hayes's fiancée, who are clearly head over heels. It's actually insulting."

"Oh, c'mon. Take a breath. It hasn't been that long. Listen, you're fighting his preconceived notions of love, which have probably been around since he was a kid, so close to twenty years or more. That's not something you can break down in a week. You're not *God*."

"Well, maybe I shouldn't *have* to fight his beliefs. Did you ever consider that?"

"You can stop anytime you like." Adele cocked her head like, *d-uh, girlfriend.*

"He confuses me. Sometimes, he...well, he acts like man in love even if he would never admit it. He puts up a good front, which is sending me mixed messages." Gia reached into her purse for her ring box and slipped it on her finger. "He gave me this wedding ring because he said I deserve something nicer than the costume ring we got in Vegas."

"Oh, my." Adele came close, bending to inspect Gia's finger. "What a rock. That must have cost a *fortune*. Actually, it cost a Fortune a fortune. See what I did there? Are you going to give it back? *Don't* give it back. You deserve it for all the pain and suffering."

Gia rolled her eyes. "I'm not keeping it if we annul. He said I could but I don't want the reminder of him if I can't have his heart."

"Girl, you're such an idealist and I love you for that. But if you don't keep that ring, I will have to slap you silly." Adele went hands on hips. "*This* is for the sisterhood."

"You should have seen his brother and Flora. It was like watching my possible future but Penn doesn't want that picture. Or maybe just not with me. It's like Marco all over again and I won't do that kind of one-sided relationship. He wants the kid and our true partnership." Gia held up air quotes. "If he says partnership *one more time*, I might have to throat punch him."

Adele sighed. "What are you going to do?"

"I think I better look into annulling a marriage and not depend on him to do it." Gia opened her laptop and searched:

how to get an annulment in Texas

how long does an annulment take

differences between annulment and divorce

can you download annulment papers

She understood from her research that an annulment was a court order basically declaring a marriage invalid. It would be as if she'd never married Penn at all. There were a few reasons listed for cause, and she thought they might best fit under fraud. Yes, it turned out she could download the form, fill it out and, for less than two hundred dollars, have it so her marriage to Penn had never happened. While Adele watched, Gia printed the form and began to fill it out at her desk.

"What are you *doing*?" Adele said, looking over her shoulder. "You're not serious."

"I don't even know his date of birth." Gia shut her eyes against the tears. "I'm married to a man and I don't know his birthday. He doesn't know mine."

"Big deal, you basically just started dating. Ask him."

"I'll need to just to fill out this form!"

"Babes, this is itty-bitty stuff." Adele gestured to the form. "You're getting hung up on the little things."

"Little? We don't even *know* each other."

"So? You'll get to know each other, all while being married and having a rock the size of Gibraltar on your finger."

She stuffed the partially filled out papers in an envelope, which she'd give to Penn. "This isn't funny. It's my *life*, and I'm falling in love with this man but he's just not going to get there with me."

"You don't know that!"

But what Gia did know, what she feared deeply in her heart, was that she was falling irrevocably in love with her husband.

Penn's playdate at the park with his nephew was wrapping up when both Hayes's and Penn's phones buzzed simultaneously. They both reached for and read the message. It was from the PI:

Oliver Webb has agreed to meet with everyone. Let's make it the Emerald Ridge Hotel this Thursday.

"That was quick," Penn said, shaking his head.

Were he Oliver, he'd be too angry to meet with the family of a father who'd never cared to even recognize his existence. Oliver seemed to be a more forgiving man than Penn. Or maybe his curiosity had won out.

"This is great," Hayes said, showing the message to Flora. "We're on our way to discovering the rest of the mystery about Archibald once we get on that land."

"It doesn't mean he'll accept the land he inherited," Penn reminded his brother. "He's just willing to meet and talk. I'm sure he realizes this isn't our fault."

"It's a start," Hayes said.

"And a chance to rehash it all, to go over how our father had a son he actually *denied*." Penn threw a look at Mateo, innocently watching them from his mother's embrace. "Can you imagine being the kind of man to turn your back on your own flesh and blood?"

"Obviously not," Hayes said, ruffling Mateo's hair. "But we don't know the whole story."

"I can't imagine any excuse that would go over well. He missed out on having a father."

That afternoon, Penn could barely concentrate on his work. In his mind, he kept replaying the picture of Gia and the man who'd been flirting with her earlier. He had plans to cook for her tonight but instead wanted to take her out. Show her off. This whole hiding-their-relationship thing wasn't going to fly with him anymore. He understood the need to keep the marriage a secret—even if it came far too close to the way his father had lived a secret life, keeping three families unaware of each other. But there was no need to pretend they weren't together. It made sense at first and they'd agreed, but maybe they didn't have to keep that part cloaked in secrecy.

It was in that moment he realized exactly how he could convince Gia to stay married. He would demonstrate how she fit seamlessly into his life.

Decision made, he picked up the phone and dialed. "I changed my mind about dinner. We're going out. Are you okay with that?"

"I do have to talk to you."

"How would you like to go to Captain's tonight? It's my mother's favorite restaurant."

"Sure. Any special occasion?"

"Yeah, I want you to meet my mother."

There was a long pause on the other end of the phone. "Oh… So, we're going public with our dating?"

"Why hide it?"

"Because that's what we decided. We're married, too, and keeping that a secret."

"And I'm okay with announcing that to the world, too, but it's your decision."

"Yes, and I'm still considering it. It's going to be difficult telling my mother I got married in a Vegas chapel. She's always wanted a church wedding."

"Damn, point taken." He honestly didn't know how to fix that.

There was a long pause. "I just realized I don't know your birthday."

"Is that important?"

"No, but it seems like something I should know as your wife. My birthday is December twentieth."

"Ah, a Christmas baby. I'm June sixth. And no comments about astrology. I know exactly who I am."

"Looks like I just missed your birthday."

"I worked through it. No big deal. It's just another day."

Best not to mention this had been ingrained in him as a child, when more often than not, his father missed the "special day." His mother had pulled out all the stops, but Penn could never get past expecting his father to show up.

"Spoken like a true Gemini," Gia chuckled. "Ha. Got you."

Penn had to laugh. "See you tonight."

He hung up, then phoned his mother. "Hey, Mom. How would you like to meet my girlfriend tonight?"

Chapter Sixteen

Captain's was a seafood restaurant on the penthouse floor of the Emerald Ridge Hotel where Penn was staying. Though upscale, there wasn't a dress code. Still, there were plenty of special occasions held here, probably due to the spectacular city view with floor-to-ceiling windows. In Penn's mind, this was a special occasion because he hoped he'd be introducing his mother to his wife. She just didn't know it yet.

Gia said she'd rather drive herself and would meet them there. Penn nabbed a table close to the windows. When his mother arrived, dressed elegantly as usual, he stood and helped her to her chair.

"This is thrilling," his mother said. "I can't believe you're dating *Gia Leonetti*! She's perfect for you."

"Well, we're new, remember? But I'm hopeful she'll realize how good we are together."

"I'm so happy for you, son. Going after what you want and never letting anyone stand in your way."

He ordered appetizers for them and a bottle of wine he thought would meet with Gia's approval. He'd learned more about wines than he'd ever thought possible, when touring Leonetti Vineyards; he'd been impressed with his wife's knowledge of everything from grape to bottle. When he looked up from the menu a moment later, Gia was walking toward them.

She looked incredible, dressed in a short, royal blue dress, her dark hair cascading around her shoulders.

He stood as she approached and gave her a quick but chaste kiss, then made the introductions.

“I’m so happy to meet you.” Penn’s mother embraced Gia. “I love your family, your vineyard, everything!”

“Thank you,” Gia said, but to Penn she seemed shy, more reserved than he’d seen her.

A mother’s approval would mean a great deal to someone like Gia. She didn’t know his mother had pretty much described *her* when suggesting the ideal woman for Penn. To put her at ease and show his support, he moved his chair closer to hers and draped an arm around her shoulders.

“How long have you two been dating?” Penn’s mother asked.

“Almost a week,” Gia said, looking to him for approval. “We met when I had a meeting with him to carry Leonetti wines in his hotels.”

“That’s true, but I’ve had my eye on her for weeks before that, ever since I first got to Emerald Ridge.”

“You didn’t tell me that,” Gia said, her cheeks flushed.

“Why do you think it was so easy to get a meeting with me?” Penn winked.

“Penn never wants to take sales pitches.” Penn’s mother waved a hand dismissively. “Always makes someone else do it. You must be *very* special.”

“She is,” Penn said, hoping he wasn’t laying it on too thick, but it was important Gia realize she’d be welcome into his family.

The calamari appetizers arrived, and naturally, he was the first to dig in. He pushed the plate toward his mother, who liked to pretend she didn’t eat.

“Like you, I’m a businesswoman,” Damaris said, taking a

sip of wine. "I respect a woman's right to have a career beyond the household. For many years, I mostly stayed home for my boys and volunteered my free time with the Junior League and other organizations. But once they were in high school, I started my own. Hearts of Fortune does philanthropic work all over the world."

Penn silently thanked his mother for making it clear he wouldn't expect his wife and the mother of his children to be tied to their home. Gia seemed impressed with his mother, asking intelligent questions and offering her own unique perspective. Dinner went so smoothly they almost closed out the restaurant. Afterwards, Penn and Gia walked his mother downstairs, and hugs were exchanged.

"I think that went well." Penn tugged Gia back to the elevator. "Something tells me she likes you."

"I like her, too. She's incredibly accomplished. No wonder she raised such a wonderful son."

"So you think I'm wonderful," Penn said, leaning down to kiss her. "Good to know."

"Penn, you know my hesitation doesn't have anything to do with who *you* are." The elevator doors opened and Gia stepped inside.

As the doors slid shut, Penn punched in the button for the penthouse. "Yeah. I get it—it's my logical and unemotional way of looking at marriage."

"That's a good way to put it." She reached to tug on his chin. "But in every other way you're the man I dreamed of marrying all my life."

Those words affected him deeply, more than he would have liked. It was a lot to live up to.

"I haven't told anyone outside of the family," he said, meeting Gia's eyes. "But I want you to understand me better. My mother adored my father—everyone thought they were a match made in heaven. Or so it seemed." He swallowed hard. "But when I was a teenager, I accidentally discovered she'd had an affair…around the time Hayes was conceived."

Gia drew in a breath and gripped his arm. "Oh, Penn. I'm so sorry."

He shook his head. "That's why we worried for a while Hayes might not be our father's biological son. But he is, so that's not the point. The *point* is, being in love is a tricky thing. My parents had plenty of ups and downs. I'm sure she had an affair because she felt lonely and neglected, and now we know why she got so little of my dad's attention." He sighed. "Don't you see? Where there's intense love, you've also got jealousy, and insecurity. All that can be destructive. One person can't own another one and romantic love tricks you into thinking you can."

Penn felt lighter after saying this. *Unburdened.* The elevator doors swished open.

"Let's not talk about this anymore," Gia said, tightly gripping his hand as they walked to his apartment.

They hadn't been inside for long before Penn noticed something square and pink out of the corner of his eye, which suspiciously resembled a cake box.

Gia walked to the kitchen. "It got here."

"What's this?" He joined her by the counter, putting his arm around her.

She looked up with a huge smile. "Special delivery from the doorman because I bribed him. It's a cake. More specifically, a birthday cake from Emerald Ridge Bakery."

"It's not my birthday." He studied the cake with blue and white icing, which read, *Happy Belated Birthday, Penn.*

"But I missed it."

She pulled out matches and a candle from her bag and lit

the candle, singing the Happy Birthday song to him like he was twelve. It was difficult not to laugh.

"You're going to make me blow out the candle, aren't you?"

"Of course," she said, threading her arms around his neck. "Make a wish!"

He blew out the candle, then reached for her butt. "Now do I get my wish?"

"No. You get your present." She unzipped her dress and let it fall to the floor. "It's me."

Damn, she *was* the perfect woman. This was a very grown-up birthday party.

"You're my present, hmm? Well, coincidentally…that *was* my wish."

He took her hand and led her to the bedroom.

Chapter Seventeen

Again, Gia had received mixed signals from Penn. He'd introduced her to his mother, shared a painful family secret, and wanted to go public with their relationship. In turn, she'd wanted to show him how much she cared by celebrating the birthday she'd missed. For now, she'd hold on to these annulment papers. Maybe Adele was right and she hadn't given this enough of a chance.

They were back in bed after eating some of his birthday cake, and she'd likely spend the night again. It had become a habit. Every time they got together, it was explosive and all-consuming, and she didn't see how she could ever give him up. Maybe it wasn't awful to have a loveless marriage if it would be anything like this. It felt very much like love, even if at times she sensed Penn creating a distance between them. He'd get a text message, rake a hand through his hair, but when she asked what was wrong, he wouldn't say. There was a part of his life he wouldn't let her into and she assumed it had to do with his newfound siblings.

And after learning that not just his father but his mother too had cheated, his reluctance to fall in love and risk such devastation made even more sense. She'd had examples of safe and healthy love her entire life, so she believed it possible. Just because she'd only dated men who didn't value her for anything but a payday, that didn't mean the right person for her wasn't out there. Maybe it could be Penn.

Adele was right when she said no one could get past twenty years of disappointment in a week. Gia had to give it more time, but *how much*? Research on annulment had led her to understand that depending on the grounds, a couple could wait as long as four years before annulling. But staying with Penn for four years was too long. By then it would be far more like a divorce and Gia would be crushed. She'd have to make her own deadlines about the annulment, and at this point, her heart would lead the way.

The next morning, she woke up again snuggled against her husband. He always threw an arm around her while she slept. She liked to spoon but eventually wound up on the other side of the bed somehow. No matter where she woke, Penn had an arm around her, even if he was sleeping on his stomach, which was often.

She rose to take a shower, get dressed and make coffee. Penn had one of those fancy machines that Gia could never understand, but she'd eventually figured out how to make a plain cup of espresso, no bells or whistles. When she brought a mug to him in the bedroom, he'd just stepped out of the shower. His golden hair was wet and he only had a towel wrapped around his torso.

She knew not to talk to him before his coffee so she handed it to him with a quick kiss. "Good morning."

"Morning," he mumbled.

He was so *not* a morning person. After he'd finished his coffee, Gia approached him.

"I want to cook for you at my condo. We always seem to wind up at your penthouse."

He shrugged into his button-up shirt. "Don't you like it here?"

"You won't really know who you're married to until you see where I've been living."

"But you said you didn't like the place." He reached for a tie from the rolling rack in his closet, which seemed to be filled with hundreds of ties.

"I said it wasn't my *choice* to move there, but I've made the best of it. And I can cook for you." She stepped close and helped him adjust the tie around his neck.

"Ah, you can help with this?" Penn looked down at her fingers working fast. "Yet another selling point."

"I learned." She decided not to tell him she'd looked up a video because Marco couldn't put on a tie if his life depended on it.

Penn didn't need any help, but she liked how he seemed to appreciate the skill.

"All right. Your place is next." He took her hand and kissed it.

"Well, I better get going…" Gia grabbed her purse and headed to the door.

She gave Penn a quick peck before she left. He didn't pull her into his arms and linger the way he usually did.

"See you tonight at my place?" she asked.

Penn lifted his wrist to glance at his watch. "No, not tonight. I have a meeting and there's a lot of stuff to iron out. I'll call you?"

A sting of disappointment went through her. "Sure," she said, wondering what had made him pull back again.

Penn was such a study in contradictions that he wasn't making any of this easy for her.

The day of the meeting with Oliver Webb arrived and even if Penn lived in the hotel, he was the last of the five siblings to arrive. For the past two days, he'd avoided people in general. That included Gia. Grumpy and uptight, he retreated into his work, the only thing in his life he could control. He hadn't even seen Gia, making one excuse after another. She'd sounded hurt over the phone. This was also one of the things he hated about relationships. He wanted someone who could accept that work would have to come first sometimes. When they had children, things would change. It seemed as though Gia would understand more than most.

After the birthday cake it seemed she wanted him to reciprocate with something equally sweet. But he'd introduced her to his *mother*, for crying out loud, what more did she want from him?

He'd done everything he could think of to show he wanted to stay married to her. Correction: he'd given her everything he could give. With any luck she'd accept what he had to offer and forget the rest of the silly romantic love ideas. The only thing he had left was to add her to his life and health insurance, not that she would need it. And, of course, they should probably draw up a postnuptial agreement. Her family would insist on it, too.

"This is the same meeting room we were in on the day we learned about our father's secret life and the terms of his will," Madeline said.

Penn thought it a boring conference room with a long glass table in the center and several uncomfortable gray chairs. He used rooms like these when he wanted to close a deal quickly and encourage everyone to leave.

"I wasn't here." Penn took a seat beside Hayes and said hello to his sisters, nodding to Madeline. "Thank you for not bringing Taffy."

"This only concerns us," Jillian said. "Our mothers don't need to be here."

"That's correct." Penn shook his head. "And Taffy's probably still licking her wounds after learning she couldn't shove Hayes out of the inheritance. That pesky DNA."

"Penn," Hayes muttered, a warning under his breath.

His brother had always tried to keep Penn's temper in check. While Penn liked avoiding people when he was angry, Hayes had better coping skills probably because he spent more time outdoors.

"I'm really sorry about my mother." Madeline studied her hands as if not wanting to meet anyone's eyes. "The DNA thing she did to Hayes was unforgiveable."

"I wouldn't call it *unforgiveable*," Hayes said. "It's understandable, in a way. Given the circumstances."

His brother, the better man.

"Anyway, I've been talking to her, and she's changing. I think she's trying, especially with the other wives."

"We don't need to talk about any of this now Madeline," Hayes said. "We're about to meet our long-lost brother."

"What do you think he looks like?" Madeline said.

"We're about to find out," Shelby said.

They all stared at the wall clock for several seconds until Hayes spoke up.

"What if he doesn't want the land? What then? Does one of us get it, or does no one?"

"We'll have to ask one of his lawyers," Penn grumbled, straightening his tie. "Tweedledee's our lawyer."

"Boy, you're in a mood," Hayes said, leaning in. "Is it girlfriend problems?"

"No, we're good."

His mood had nothing to do with Gia. She was, after all, the woman for him. With all the compassion she'd given, he still hoped she'd understand and give him some leeway.

When Penn looked up, a man stood in the doorway, as if hesitant to enter. Penn didn't blame him. He'd bet this was

Oliver Webb in the flesh. The family resemblance shocked him. He had Archibald's deep-set blue eyes.

"I'm Oliver," he said.

For a moment, nobody moved, then Penn rose to meet him halfway.

"Penn Fortune." He shook Oliver's hand, then introduced everyone. "Good to meet you. Have a seat."

"This meeting is a long time coming," Hayes said, shaking the man's hand. "I always thought I only had one brother."

"And I always believed I was an only child." The words sat between them like a grenade.

What must it have been like to grow up without a father, and later learning of his immense wealth? Penn would carry the anger for a long while.

"I always thought I was an only child, too," Madeline said. "We're so sorry this happened to you, to *all* of us. You deserved to be acknowledged as a Fortune while Archibald was still alive."

Everyone murmured their agreement.

Oliver nodded but sat a healthy distance from everyone else. "The way I understand it, y'all had nothing to do with this, so I don't blame any of you. I might envy you a little, but that's *different*. See, I've wanted answers my whole life and this is more of a bombshell than I ever imagined. I was worried I'd discover I was the son of someone serving time in prison."

"Did your mother ever tell you about her past before she died?" Jillian asked curiously.

"She died ten years ago when I was nineteen, but whenever I had questions, she'd brush them off. She'd always asked me not to look into her past. After she died, I honored her wishes because I thought she knew best."

"You have family on your mother's side, too," Shelby informed him. "When we first started looking for you, we learned your mother had an elderly aunt, Jeralyn Ward. She's in a memory care unit in Bisonville. We visited her and she's barely lucid but hanging in there."

"I didn't know of any relatives on my mother's side." Oliver's eyes softened and he gave the hint of a smile. "I'll have to visit her."

"Yes, we'll give you all the information," Jillian murmured.

Penn cleared his throat. "Will you accept the land inheritance from our father?"

Hayes elbowed him, like maybe he should have given the man a little more time. But Penn wanted answers only Oliver could provide and he didn't see why he shouldn't get straight to the point. To Penn, Oliver seemed reserved, almost reluctant to be here. Not that he blamed him. They were all complete strangers. At least the rest of them had had a few months to get used to the idea they had siblings they hadn't known about. Oliver would have to catch up to them.

"The land's valuable but more importantly it could provide us all with some answers," Madeline said and Penn gave her a grateful nod.

"Yeah, we all need peace," Hayes chimed in.

"I don't know." Oliver slowly shook his head. "Not to be rude, but I don't need my father's inheritance. I've done well for myself and don't need anything from him. If he couldn't acknowledge me when he was alive, I don't see the point now."

"I get it," Penn said, pulling out his negotiating skills. It was time to close this deal. "I made my own money, too. Maybe you're like me, trying to understand Archibald. What kind of man feels the needed to juggle three different families and keep them all secret from one another?"

All three of his sisters gave Penn grateful smiles. He'd put into words everything they'd hammered into him from the start. This would never truly be over until they could get on that land Archibald found so important to leave for Oliver. They'd all done their part to find him, and now it was up to Oliver to join them.

"I don't know." Oliver hesitated. "Let me have some time. I'll let you know..."

The meeting came to a close, Oliver excusing himself and thanking everyone for meeting with him and giving him the information on his aunt.

"Well, that went well." Hayes took off his ever-present cowboy hat and raked a hand through his hair. "He hates us because we grew up with our father and he didn't."

"It could have been worse," Penn said. "He listened."

"I wanted to hug him," Madeline said, wiping a tear from her eye. "But it didn't feel right."

"Yeah, I'm not sure he would've been open to that," Jillian slipped an arm around her half-sister, pulling her into a hug. "But I hope he changes his mind about the land."

"We need to give him more time," Penn said.

It occurred to him it was exactly a week ago today that he'd met Gia in his office in Las Vegas and wound up marrying her. *One week*, which was all the time he'd asked her to consider staying married.

He still didn't know whether he'd ever discover what was on the land his father left Oliver, or for that matter, if he'd stay married to Gia.

He was hanging, waiting for others to make decisions that would affect the rest of his life.

For a businessman, it was an untenable place to be.

Chapter Eighteen

Afterward, Penn invited Hayes upstairs to his penthouse for a cold beer and some commiserating over how the introduction to their half brother hadn't gone as everyone had hoped. Penn *hadn't* closed the deal despite his best efforts. Oliver had to think about it.

"Is that birthday cake?" Hayes pointed.

"Yep." Penn laughed. "Gia ordered it for me since she missed my birthday."

"You won the girlfriend lottery with her, didn't you?" Hayes took a pull from his beer.

"You don't know the half of it." Penn snorted. "I am *extremely* lucky."

Hayes moved to the sectional couch and switched the flatscreen on to the game. "I've got a few minutes before I've got to get home to Flora and Mateo. Let's think about something else besides land, money, PIs and lost siblings."

"Let me call my secretary and leave a message first." Penn spoke into his cell. "Remind me tomorrow to look into drawing up a postnuptial agreement. I keep forgetting. Flag it as important."

"Already?" Hayes hit Mute on the TV and chuckled. "And don't you mean *pre*nuptial?"

For a moment, a beat of silence passed between them. He hadn't intended for this to slip out, and he'd promised Gia to keep it from the family. They were only supposed to be dating, not married.

Penn raked a hand through his hair and winced. “Uh, yeah. No, I meant post.”

Hayes’s eyes suddenly went the size of a mosquito’s and he sat up straight. *“What?”*

“Don’t tell anyone.” Penn tipped back on his heels, now eager to spill his guts. “But I’m married to Gia Leonetti.”

“No, you’re not.”

“Actually, yes, I am.” Penn grabbed his beer and joined Hayes on the couch.

“When the hell did *this* happen?”

“A week ago. We got married in Vegas at my hotel’s chapel. It was one of those spur-of-the-moment, I’ve-taken-leave-of-my-senses kind of things. We were both a little impaired after drinking some amazing wine. We thought we’d get it annulled when we got home, but…well… I want to stay married.”

“Of course you do.” Hayes grinned. “I’ll be damned. No wonder you looked like you’d tear Michael’s head off for flirting with Gia. And here I thought you were over-the-top possessive. I was getting ready to have a come-to-Jesus moment with you.”

A flash of irritation sliced through Penn. “What do you mean? I’m not *possessive.*”

Hayes snorted. “It sure looked that way. And it’s natural to be a little jealous of the woman you love, especially when you’ve made a commitment to each other.”

“I’m not possessive and I’m *not* in love, either.” Penn stretched out his legs and crossed them at the ankles.

“Then why do you want to *stay* married?” Hayes squinted, as if he’d been given an algebra word problem to solve.

“You’ve seen her. She’s the perfect woman.”

Hayes cocked his head. “But…you don’t *love* her?”

"Look, I'm not interested in all those ups and downs in a relationship. Maybe it works for you and Flora, but what I want is something solid and unbreakable. No offense, but I think love is a big sham. Totally overrated. What I've suggested to her is a marriage based on mutual respect, similar backgrounds and upbringings. A true partnership. Those are the things that matter and keep a marriage strong."

Hayes snorted. "And how fast did she want to hitch her wagon to yours after all that sweet sexy talk?"

Penn scowled. "She's still considering it."

"Uh-huh." Hayes nodded. "Color me not surprised."

"What am I supposed to do? Just let her go?" Penn splayed his hands wide.

"No, I see your dilemma."

"I'm trying to talk her into it, but I'm not sure it's working. We said we'd give it a week then decide if we should annul."

"And time's up."

"Yeah. Either she's going to serve me with annulment papers or move in with me." He tipped his bottle. "I've already made some room in the closet and cleared out a dresser drawer for her."

Hayes nearly spit out his beer. "Dude, let me be the one to break this to you. You're going to have to give her the entire closet."

"Where will my clothes go?"

"No one cares." Hayes shook his head. "It's not like you don't have a lot of space. Use another bedroom and that closet. You have a lot to learn about marriage."

"So, I have to get dressed in another room? That's what you're telling me?"

"That's the least of it," his brother informed him. "You're going to need to try to like what she likes, or at least *some* of the time. There's a lot of compromising in marriage."

"I really hate compromising," Penn grumbled. "I do it sometimes in a business deal and I always feel cheated."

But Hayes was correct. If he wanted to think of this marriage as another contract, another successful business deal, he might have to compromise a little.

"I don't think you're ready for marriage," his brother said.

"That's too bad because I'm already married." Penn closed his eyes and pinched the bridge of his nose. "I'll have to figure this out because we're great on paper. We make sense."

"Why, you charmer. And you're actually going to have her sign a postnup?"

Penn shrugged. "I'm sure her family will want one, too. We're both wealthy. It's just practical."

"Yeah, and very cold."

"It doesn't have to be. You don't think Flora's family will want *you* to sign one?"

"I don't think so. We have a son together. What's mine is ours."

"Okay, if that's what you think is best." Penn leaned back, giving up.

"The truth is I was like you, thinking Flora and I could be practical about our relationship. You know, co-parent our child together. Then I fell in love so I asked her to marry me. I know I don't want to start a marriage already thinking it could end."

Hayes didn't have to *think* that—he should already *know* it could happen and likely would. Maybe not soon, but someday. Penn stopped short of telling his brother that his marriage might not last. He didn't have the heart to burst his bubble like that.

"I mean, look at our examples. Two parents who were in love but they both cheated. Sure, one cheated worse than the other one, but we both know they had reasoning that must have made sense to them. With Mom, hindsight being twenty-twenty, it's obvious she felt neglected. She *was*. Our father? No idea what excuse he could come up with except the fact he was greedy. It wasn't enough to have one happy family. He needed three."

"Apparently he stopped at three because, you know, poor Oliver."

Penn nodded. "Glad I'm not the only one who feels guilty."

"Agreed, our father screwed up but *I* don't intend to. I'm going to work hard to keep my family together and I'm never going to take Flora for granted. My family will always be my priority and I vow to have only one. But damn, I didn't know you were this jaded about love."

"Admit it, love is messy. What happens when you have a huge argument or fight? Lots of tears and yelling. Broken hearts. Breakup time, right?"

Hayes crinkled his brow. "No, that's *makeup* time. And makeup sex is the best ever."

Makeup sex was not what Penn called fixing a problem. More like ignoring one. Every time he'd fought with a girlfriend, it felt like one nail in the coffin, no matter how great the sex was after. But then again, he'd never been motivated enough to stick around.

"I think I need a better introduction to your wife," Hayes said. "You two should come over for dinner sometime."

"Yep, just name the day."

Hayes unmuted the TV and the sports announcer's voice boomed with excitement. The batter was up and the bases were loaded.

Like the player up, Penn wanted a grand slam.

Gia checked her phone after she cleaned up the dinner dishes. Sometimes it accidentally slipped to buzz instead of ring and she missed alerts. But there were still zero messages from Penn after the last one in which he'd told her he couldn't see her because he had a meeting with his siblings to talk about their inheritance. Apparently, it had been confirmed—the man who came to Leonetti Vineyards searching for his mother was in fact the missing Fortune brother, Oliver Webb. It must be so strange to not know your own biological family. Gia couldn't imagine how that felt.

Still, Penn had been avoiding her for a couple of days and while she understood he was under a lot of stress, it wasn't cool to ignore her. They'd become so close and spent so much time together recently that now she missed him. But she wondered if this was what a marriage to him would be like. He'd simply check in when he wanted to, and check out when he wanted to, too. Nope, that wasn't going to work for her.

The doorbell rang and she opened the door to find Penn, holding a bouquet of roses. He looked more dressed down than she'd ever seen him. He wasn't wearing a tie, but jeans and a short-sleeved polo shirt. She had to do a double take. This was the casual version of her husband. So, he wasn't always in a suit. Good to know.

"Penn!" Though her heart skipped a beat at the sight of him, she inwardly cringed. She wasn't exactly ready to entertain anyone, wearing an old "Vino" T-shirt and yoga pants. "I expected you to call first."

"I'm sorry." He stepped forward to take her into his arms. "I just wanted to see you."

She found it difficult to be irked with him when he smelled so good. She palmed his jaw. "I'm glad you're here. I've missed you."

He took her left hand in his and threaded his fingers through hers. "Hey, you're wearing my ring."

The words sent a sweet ache to her heart because he sounded so pleased. She tugged him into her condo.

"God, I've missed you, too. It's been a lousy couple of days." He followed her into the kitchen.

"Why, what happened?" Gia filled a vase with water and took the red roses from him.

"Our half brother, Oliver, actually showed up at the meeting." Penn raked a hand through his hair. "Let's just say he's not thrilled with any of us. Yeah, he knows it's not *our* fault our father was a cheating bastard. But I believe he also sees everything he missed. He grew up without a father, and a mother who didn't want him digging into his past. Now we're not even sure he'll take his share of the inheritance—land where we might find answers to more of our family secrets."

So much for shutting her out of his family drama. Now she understood why he'd been in a funk and hadn't wanted to hang out. Poor Penn, of course he would feel some shame for his father's mistakes and the way he'd conducted himself as a man, even if he had nothing to do with it. Still, in a real marriage, couples shared situations like this, and the fact that he hadn't made her feel included made her worry that the emotional intimacy she craved with him would never be where she needed it to be.

"I wish you'd told me because I would have listened."

He lifted a shoulder. "Didn't want to bother you."

"But that's what a marriage is, Penn. If you want to be *partners*, as you say, you need to let me know about these things."

"I know, you're right. I'm sorry. Not used to having someone that I can talk to about these unpleasant family things."

As if he suddenly realized he was in her home, he spun around and took it all in. "This is your place."

Her kitchen was connected to the family room by a gray

granite kitchen island. A more formal dining room lay ahead and the bedrooms were down a hallway. She didn't need all this space but somehow she'd filled it.

"Thankfully, I straightened up today, because I wasn't expecting you." Hand on hip, she playfully stuck out her tongue.

She hoped he noticed that even if the condo's walls were beige and the window treatments matched, she'd put the Leonetti stamp on it all. The couch was green and plush, so comfortable a person could easily take a nap on it. Bright and colorful red, yellow, purple and orange throw pillows, along with Tuscan art on the walls, filled her with pride. She'd scouted galleries and antique shops for the perfect pieces. Framed photos of her family were everywhere—on the countertop, the end tables, built-ins and coffee tables.

"If you were to blindfold me and take me into an apartment to pick yours, I would have known this was the one."

"You know me that well, do you?" Grinning, she tugged him into the other room.

He sat and stretched on the couch. "What is this trickery? How is this so comfortable but still looks like a showpiece?"

"It's a mystery," she teased. "I hope you're not hungry because I already had dinner."

He pulled her down to sit next to him. "Look, I don't expect you to cook for me every night like a little 1960s wife."

"Don't worry, I won't. But I'll cook for you when I damn well please."

"Oh, okay, sweetheart," he chuckled. "Whatever you say."

"So, about those annulment papers…" she began.

"Let's not talk about that right now," he said, taking her hand. "We have plenty of time for all that."

"Okay, but it's been a week and we should talk about it." She squeezed his hand. "Penn, I need you to at least be open to the possibility you could fall in love otherwise this won't work."

"I'll show you how it can work. We can work. Could I bargain for another week?" He slid her a panty-melting grin. "I need more time to convince you. To be fair, I've had my attention on the hot mess that's my current family."

"That's fine but there's some stuff we need to talk about," she told him.

"Hit me with it."

"What do we actually have in common? I mean, besides the fact we both have money, big families and are fans of Leonetti wine?"

"Well…" It seemed as if he was really considering the question. "It's definitely something to discuss."

"In a healthy relationship, we have to share some hobbies and interests. My parents used to play chess together for hours. Our family used to have board game night."

"Mine, too."

She quirked a brow. "What's your favorite board game?"

"You really have to ask?" He winked.

"Monopoly," she guessed. "Mine's Clue."

"Movies." She snapped her fingers.

He leaned his head back. "Yes, love them."

She smirked. "Well, good. You're not a weirdo. What *kind* of movie do you prefer?"

"Okay." He gave her a look from under hooded eyes. "Don't laugh."

"I would never." Gia put a hand to her chest. "But is it *Die Hard*?"

"Star Wars." He lowered his head, covered his face and said this as if admitting to a guilty pleasure. "*All* of them."

"How predictable." Gia elbowed him. "You're a true millennial."

"Hey, so are you. And you said you wouldn't laugh." He grabbed her arm but was laughing, too.

"I have a brother, so I've watched them all, but they're not my favorites."

"It's rom-coms, isn't it?" He said with a wince. "Well, nobody's perfect."

"*True crime* and I like to take notes." She tossed her hair back. "It's always the wife, unless it's the husband. Would you like to see my notes on how to get away with the perfect murder?"

"About that annulment…" Penn chuckled, playing with a lock of her hair.

"I'm joking." She grinned. "Actually, the classics are my favorites. *Casablanca*, *The Philadelphia Story*, *An Affair to Remember*."

"You can never go wrong with *Casablanca*." Penn tipped an imaginary hat. "Of all the joints in all the world, she has to walk into mine."

It was a fairly good impersonation. "Well, not a joint, but your office."

"And I knew I was in trouble the minute you did."

"You didn't even see me walk in the room, too busy with something on your desk!" She laughed.

"As I told you the other day, I'd had my eye on you before we were even introduced." He met her gaze, his own eyes deep and intense. "But when I saw you up close and personal, I felt like I'd been hit over the head with a bat."

"You had ulterior motives. Maybe that's why I felt like I'd walked into the lion's den." She reached to tug on his shirt collar. "To be honest, you scared me a little bit with your intensity. I've never been more attracted to a man, or ever in my entire life been the first to *proposition* anyone."

"We'd been drinking." He took her hand from his collar and kissed her palm.

"Yeah, my inhibitions were lowered." She took her hand back. "But they're not right now. I can see where this is headed. We do this an awful lot."

He gave her a slow smile. "I have zero complaints."

"Me, either, but we should see how long we can be in a room together without going at it. Restraint."

Penn squinted his eyes as though thoroughly confused. *"Why?"*

"To see what we have in common besides great sex." She took the remote control and the hidden flat-screen rolled up. "Movie time."

The TV was one more of Marco's many techie toys, but she liked it, too. So did Adele, and on their girls' night they'd watch a parade of movies while eating popcorn. Gia clicked to the movie section and found *Casablanca.*

As the credits rolled, Penn leaned back among the pillows. "Okay. Let's do this. It's been a while, Bogie."

Gia curled up in Penn's arms because cuddling was not off the table. But as the movie went on, her eyes drooped heavier and she fell asleep before the movie ended. She blamed the comfy couch, site of many an accidental nap. Fighting to keep her eyes open, she briefly looked over at Penn. It wasn't her imagination to see a certain telltale wetness in his eyes. This movie always made her cry, too. The sacrificial love got to her every time.

In the morning, she woke up in her bed. Alone. Still wearing all her clothes. Penn had left her a note:

I wouldn't have given Ilsa up. Rick was an idiot. See you tonight.

Gia smiled. He'd passed the movie test, and this was a pretty good note. It would remain to be seen if he'd ever change his mind about love.

Chapter Nineteen

At the office the next morning, Gia got her calls done early and had Adele order lunch from Francesca's Bar and Grill so they could chat as they usually did when there were no pressing appointments.

"Penn came over last night and we watched *Casablanca.*" Gia took a bite of her Chinese chicken salad.

"Oh, wow, that's a true test."

Gia waved her hand dismissively. "Actually, that's *An Affair to Remember.* If a guy zones out on that one, it tells me something. And it's not good."

She was kind of afraid to watch that one with Penn. Some guys got a bit upset at the fact the heroine didn't show up for their meeting, neglecting the fact she was in a wheelchair.

Did she ever hear of a phone? If you're not going to show up, call!

Wait. They had phones at that time in history, right? This one was usually the kiss of death for Gia.

Adele looked up from her sandwich. "Did the poor guy know this was a test?"

"No, they never do." She rubbed her hands together diabolically.

"I can see why you'd want your husband to pass this test with flying colors."

"The point is, I'm looking for things we have in common

besides a great sex life. That's vital for a long and successful marriage. We can't have sex twenty-four seven. People have lives, ya know."

Adele threw her napkin down. "Please, girl, I can't sit here and listen to you *complaining* about all this great sex you're having. Have a little consideration."

"Okay, sorry." Gia smiled. "I'm not complaining. It's just—"

Her bestie put up her palm and her neck swiveled back. "No."

They ate in silence for a few seconds and then Adele spoke up. "Have y'all talked about moving in together?"

Gia poised the fork halfway to her mouth. "*Move in* together?"

Adele deadpanned. "That thing couples do when they're married. It helps conserve, not that y'all need to save on rent but think about the rest of us. Your carbon footprint."

"Oh, you're right. I hadn't considered it. It's not like I love living in my condo, but isn't it a bit presumptuous to invite myself to move in with him?"

"I see, so he hasn't mentioned it."

"No," Gia said, suddenly wondering why he hadn't.

He was the one who wanted to *stay* married. Shouldn't they at least try living together for a *weekend*, a trial by fire?

"Fine. I'm going to suggest it, even if we're already spending nearly every night together."

"Good call. Just remember, it's different when you live together and play house," Adele cautioned. "You go to sleep every night and wake up every morning and all your stuff is already there. You'll have to blend all your stuff. Two coffee machines, two toasters, not to mention all the furniture."

"Oh, I don't want to give up my furniture," Gia moaned.

"Don't blame you."

Later that afternoon, as the workday drew to a close, she texted Penn:

Have you considered a trial run of our marriage?

Penn wrote back:

I thought that's what we were doing. By the way, whenever you want to move in, I cleared out the closet for you and some dresser drawers.

Well, that was easy. He hadn't mentioned it before but the *entire* closet?

The whole closet? she asked.

I figure you need the room more than I do. My clothes are in the spare room.

Smiling, she texted, That's incredibly generous but I probably don't need the entire closet.

You have it if you want it. Whatever you want, came his reply.

Gia wanted to whine that she preferred her apartment if nothing else because of the homey decor and how hard she'd worked to make it a home. But the truth was that the Emerald Ridge Hotel was quite a bit closer to her fifth-floor office. Nothing was too far in downtown Emerald Ridge, but she'd literally be able to walk to work. The idea tempted her, and it was only temporary, so she wasn't giving up her condo and all the cool things in it. Even Penn loved her couch. But her condo and couch would still be here if this didn't work out, or if they chose to combine their households somewhere else...like her family home.

She could make her case for Penn moving in with her, but she figured maybe she'd compromise now and save her passionate pleas for moving to the Leonetti family mansion for later. Gia picked up the phone and dialed Penn.

"Okay," she said. "I'll pack a few things and we can give it another week. But really, I won't need the *whole* closet."

"The thing is, Gia, I remember you saying you bent over backwards for your ex. You moved to the condo because that's what *he* wanted. I just want to be clear—this should happen only if it's what you want, too. No pressure."

She couldn't adequately express how much this concession meant to her. No one had ever considered her feelings first.

"So…are you okay with moving in?"

"Yes," she said without hesitation. "We should do this as part of our evaluation to stay married."

"Great." There was the sound of tapping in the background and Penn cleared his throat. "Am I still seeing you tonight?"

"Yes, come to my place. I can cook for you tonight as long as you show up on time."

"I don't have any more meetings, so I'll be there by seven if not sooner."

When Gia got home, she set her groceries down, kicked off her heels, tied on her apron and went to work. While it was good Penn didn't expect her to cook for him every night, she was old-fashioned enough to want to do it occasionally. Besides, she was fortunately a good cook, according to Mama. Ironically, however, her best dish was paella, which she'd learned to cook while traveling in Spain the year after college graduation.

She loved the combination of so many ingredients and the challenge of creating such a spectacular dish. The key to the perfect paella was the socarrat, the caramelized crispy rice at the bottom of the pan. Gia used authentic ingredients like sofrito, saffron and bomba rice. She then added tomato, flat green beans, chicken and lima beans to the mix. By the time Penn arrived, the entire apartment gave off a delicious scent.

He kissed her in the doorway. "Why does it smell so great in here?"

She tugged him into the kitchen. "Paella, my special dish."

"Isn't that a Spanish dish? I don't think I've ever had it before."

"In that case, you're in for such a treat!" She'd set the table with her best dishes and his roses for her centerpiece.

They sat on the small round table across from each other.

"This is delicious," Penn said after taking a few bites. "How'd you learn to make this dish?"

"After college, I traveled in Europe for a while and stayed with a friend's family in Madrid. The grandmother loved teaching me how to cook the authentic Spanish way. In return, I shared some Leonetti family recipes." She winked at him. "Shh. Don't tell my nonna."

"I traveled to Europe after college, too. Must have just missed you." Penn scratched at his neck and loosened his tie.

She almost had an aneurysm—a loose tie was *so* sexy on him. "Did you spend any time in Spain?"

He helped himself to some water from the pitcher and downed the glass. "Not much time, no."

"Are you okay?" She noticed he'd rolled up the sleeves of his shirt to his forearms and it wasn't hot in here.

"I think so," he said, tugging at the neck of his collar. "Hey, by any chance is there any saffron in this?"

A terrible sense of foreboding hit Gia square in the chest. "Yes, it's one of the key ingredients! Why?"

He cursed. "I'm allergic."

"To *saffron*? Oh my God, Penn! How could you not tell me you're allergic?"

"It's not like I'm allergic to peanuts or anything commonplace. Who cooks with saffron?"

"Lots of Spanish people!"

"And you're Italian. Don't worry, I'm not anaphylactic or anything. I'm not going to die." He tore his shirt off.

Pink welts had formed on his chest and around his upper arms. They seemed to be spreading.

"I was just kidding about true crime! You believe me, don't you? I don't want you to die!"

"Calm down," Penn said, downing another glass of water. "I'm not going to die and you're not helping."

Gia didn't know what to do and panic rose in her at the thought she'd even accidentally hurt her husband. Humiliation was not far behind. She should have asked for any allergies before she cooked for him. That was cooking 101.

"Do you have any Benadryl?" Penn asked. "I think that will help."

Gia ran to the medicine cabinet and started riffling through, finding very little besides her skin and hair products. She didn't even have headache medicine since she'd rarely had one after Marco left. At this moment, she was clearly cursed for being so damn healthy.

"I don't have anything!" she yelled when she walked back into the kitchen. "Should I call an ambulance?"

Penn looked at her like she'd suggested the earth was flat. "Maybe instead you could go to the store and get some Benadryl."

"Yes, of course, I could do that!" She grabbed her purse but in her panic, she upset several items on the counter and they all fell to the ground with a loud bang.

"Gia, for the love of God, would you calm the hell down?" Penn yelled.

"Don't you dare yell at me!" she yelled. "I'm trying to save your life."

"Not without your car keys, you're not." He held them up. "And I'm going with you."

Penn threw his shirt back on loosely, not tucked in, the sleeves rolled up and the collar open.

On the way to the pharmacy, Gia groaned. "I'm so sorry! Is there anything else you're allergic to?"

"Panic, apparently," he muttered. "You're making this worse. How is it you were so helpful when I made an emergency landing and now you're hysterical? It's just an allergic reaction."

The primary difference was that the airplane hadn't been her fault, but the same couldn't be said about the saffron. She couldn't bear to see Penn in such agony. Because, damn it, she loved him and she'd hurt him without realizing it. She'd never forgive herself.

"The difference is this is my fault, Penn. I fed you."

"It's not your fault, sweetheart."

"You're just trying to make me feel better."

After picking up the Benadryl, Gia had the presence of mind to ask the pharmacist for advice—an idea that struck her while her thoughts were spiraling, but felt brilliant in the moment. Once they arrived back home, she flew into Florence Nightingale mode, remembering all the times her mother had nursed her after a cold or flu. As the youngest in the family, Gia had never really had to take care of anyone, and the unfamiliarity of tending to her husband had thrown her into a tailspin. She was used to knowing what to do—how to fix things. Now, at least, she had this. Penn took the antihistamine, and she put him to bed, propping pillows all around him and making a cold compress for the welts. Within an hour, the swelling had noticeably reduced, and a sense of calm settled over them both.

"Thank you," Penn said when she applied a wet towel to his head. "This really helps."

"I'm so sorry," Gia said, biting her lower lip to hold back the tears.

"I know, sweetheart. That's clear." He took her hand and threaded his fingers through hers.

"I should have asked for any food allergies before I cooked for you."

"And I'm sorry I yelled." Penn lifted the towel to peek at her. "We had our first fight."

"I know."

"We did good, though," Penn said. "No name-calling, no hostility or mean-spirited insults. Just a lot of chaos and confusion, which is natural given what happened."

She lay back among the pillows and laid her head on his shoulder. "Agreed. And I felt safe with you even when you were yelling."

It was the same kind of passionate arguing that happened in the Leonetti home from time to time followed by apologies and tender agreements.

For Gia, this felt a lot like love, but would she survive the fallout if he never felt the same?

Chapter Twenty

On the weekend she moved into Penn's apartment, Gia shared the elevator going up with someone who looked familiar. She couldn't place the name though it was on the tip of her tongue. The woman looked to be in her mid- to late fifties, with stylishly cut and layered blond hair. She was dressed impeccably in an Yves Saint Laurent soft pink pantsuit. Quite classy and reminded Gia of Penn's mother, who looked equally sophisticated.

"Hello," Gia said as she stepped inside, holding her potted fern.

The movers had already taken up several boxes of her clothes, shoes and toiletries but none of her furniture. This was only a trial run, after all. She reminded herself of this daily to assuage her nerves. Moving in together was a *big deal* and carried with it such a weight of hope for the future. Especially for her. Maybe she'd stay married to Penn after all. The annulment papers were still unsigned in her bag and she'd forced herself to stop thinking about them.

"Hello," the woman said smoothly, holding out her hand. "I'm Taffy Fortune."

"Nice to meet you. Gia Leonetti." Gia moved the plant to offer her hand to Taffy.

"Of Leonetti Vineyards?"

“Yes, that’s my family.” Gia smiled like she did when pride for her family took over her whole face.

Unfortunately, the only thing she knew about this woman was that she was part of the Fortune family scandal. One of the three wives, she understood, who’d been tricked by Penn’s father, Archibald.

“Are you moving into the building?” Taffy asked, pushing the button for the sixth floor.

“Yes.”

Gia held tight to her plant. She didn’t want the woman to know she was moving in with *Penn*. But it seemed from what Penn said that the wives weren’t all super close with each other so maybe Penn’s mother didn’t have to know.

She’d have to mention to Penn that she’d run into Taffy Fortune.

“It’s a great building. What floor?” Taffy prodded, as the elevator came to a stop on the fourth floor.

“Um…” Gia said, and when the elevator doors slid open, there stood Damaris Fortune.

Again, she was dressed in haute couture, fashionable enough to walk down a runway, her makeup and hair impeccable.

“Gia, dear!” Damaris stepped in and kissed Gia’s cheek. “Coming to see Penn? Oh, he’s hopeless with plants! I’ve talked him into the fake ones.”

“She’s moving into the building,” Taffy explained.

“Wonderful. That will be convenient for you and Penn. Taffy, this is my son’s girlfriend.” Damaris set a hand on either of Gia’s shoulders, as if presenting her.

“Oh, really?” Taffy zeroed in on Gia, assessing carefully. “She’s lovely.”

“Isn’t she?”

First time for everything, including having two mothers talk about her as if she wasn't there. Gia forced a smile.

"Floor?" Taffy repeated to Gia, finger hovering over the button. "You were going up. We'll come down after you go up to yours."

Her mind raced. If she told them the penthouse they would make certain conclusions. She would rather they not find out she was temporarily moving in with Penn.

"Eighth floor," Gia said, hating herself for lying.

She got off the elevator on the eighth floor and waved to the women as the doors slid shut. She waited until the elevator went down and came back up again.

Lying was exhausting.

The movers were hauling boxes into the bedroom when Penn heard Gia let herself inside with the code he'd given her. He got up, setting aside his laptop where he'd been looking over some blueprints for the new resort hotel in Italy.

"Hey. They're in there." He gestured toward their bedroom.

When they'd arrived, he'd simply led them to the bedroom and pointed out the closet. From what he could see, the boxes were labeled Clothes and Shoes. But there were also books and framed photos, some jewelry and of course all the detritus that came with being a woman. He didn't care. He welcomed all of it. Marriage was about compromise and he was ready to make some compromises. As long as she would make the compromise to a partnership and not a love match. It went both ways.

She set the plant down on the end table. "Penn… I just ran into your mother on the elevator."

He rubbed the stubble on his chin. "Did you tell her you're moving in with me?"

"No, I thought we decided *not* to do that."

"Yeah. You're right not to say anything yet," he said.

"But I feel horrible because I lied. See, I made the mistake of admitting that I was moving into this building. So, I said I was on the eighth floor. Then I got off and just stayed there until the elevator went down and came back up."

Penn chuckled. Ever since the night of the allergic reaction, he'd seen Gia in a different light. An even *better* one. She was no longer perfection personified but just as fallible as he saw himself. She was self-deprecating and funny as hell when she wanted to be. It made her, if anything, more endearing. She'd completely freaked at the realization she'd hurt him. He didn't think anyone besides his own mother had ever cared that much about his pain and discomfort. And then, he came to the realization that Gia had never before taken care of someone the way she had cared for him that night. Though the hives were painful, they were almost worth it to see that side of her. His instincts were right. She'd make a great mother to his children.

He took her into the crook of his arms. "It's okay. She'll understand and forgive you."

"Now Taffy also thinks I live on that floor. She was there, too." She buried her face in his shoulder and made a small sound.

He froze. "She was where? Taffy? Taffy *Fortune*?"

Of course it was Taffy Fortune. Who else had such a ridiculous first name?

"She was on the elevator, too. She and your mother were going somewhere together. They seem to be...getting along."

"What did Taffy say to you? I want to know. I'll have words with her if she said anything even remotely insulting."

Gia blinked. "She was perfectly nice, actually."

All the hot air went out of him. "Okay, good."

"You don't like her, do you?" Gia cocked her head. "Tell

me why, other than the obvious. Because your mother seems to have forgiven her. It's not her fault your father lied to her. He lied to all of his wives."

"That's not why," Penn said, heading to the kitchen. "She's a piece of work, that woman. She wanted to cut Hayes out of the inheritance. It would have been more money for everyone else if she didn't have to split the pie too many ways. She's selfish and self-absorbed. I'm not even sure Madeline likes her. Once Taffy learned my mother had an affair, she tried to use that and suggest Hayes might not be a Fortune by blood. She insisted Hayes have his paternity tested. Madeline told us she's trying to improve, so maybe that's true."

Thank God Taffy had been wrong about his brother, and maybe some good had come out of the whole debacle, knowing Hayes was his full biological brother.

"I can see you're very passionate about the people you love."

He couldn't argue when she looked at him with those big, dark eyes that always stirred something wild in him.

"You could say that. I guess I'm protective of my family, and that's you now, too. You're my *wife.*"

"Your secret wife."

"For now." He kissed her, a long and deep kiss that only scratched the surface of his desire. "And given what I've been through with my father, I'm not enjoying the secret. I'm leaving it up to you to decide when we tell *everyone* we're married."

"But…if we stay married, are we going to tell everyone the unvarnished truth?"

"Ah, you mean the Lovers Lane Chapel and all the wine?" Penn winced. "Hmm. Maybe we should leave that part out? I want you protected and safe from any harsh judgment."

He meant it with every part of him. Waking up married in

Vegas carried with it certain implications and he was painfully aware they'd be far worse for Gia than him. It wasn't fair, but true. His reputation would take the hit far easier.

"It's definitely not the Leonetti way. We have big church weddings, but I learned something recently I'd never known before. Papa Enzo's grandparents, the ones that came to America and started Leonetti wines, were an arranged marriage. They didn't know each other well."

Penn quirked a brow, hoping this was a good thing, because it seemed to be something to add in the column to support staying married.

"And…was it a good marriage?"

"From everything I've ever heard, they were soul mates. Together all the time, and a perfect match."

"See? That's what I'm talking about! That's us." Penn reached for her.

She didn't resist, curling her arms around his neck and gazing up at him.

"But they were in love. Maybe not at first, but that's why they never spent a single night apart and built a family and a business. According to Papa, love grew because everything else was right."

He understood what Gia wanted and what she hoped he'd say. She needed him to admit that a marriage couldn't truly work without romantic love. What she longed to hear was that he could fall in love with her.

But love, for him, came with too high a cost.

"Hey, we're all done here," one of the movers called out.

"Thanks for your help," Penn said, grabbing his wallet to tip them.

Together, he and Gia saw them to the door. Closing the door, Penn turned to her. "Were those guys our first guests?"

Gia laughed. "Not sure they count."

He followed her into their bedroom, strolling behind, trying to give her space.

"It already smells better in here."

The light flowery scent was *all* Gia.

Later that day, after they'd called for takeout and eaten it out of the containers while watching Netflix, they went to bed. Except this time going to bed meant brushing teeth side by side. He watched as his wife went through her nighttime routine of washing her face and applying creams of various kinds. All he could say was she smelled even better by the time she was finished.

He usually wore nothing but his underwear to bed, sometimes a pair of sweatpants. When Gia emerged from the walk-in closet where she'd changed, she wore silky white, short lingerie. He nearly swallowed his tongue. She looked better than she did *naked* and this said something. When she crawled into bed next to him, he pulled her into his arms and pressed a kiss against her temple.

She whispered into his neck, "Just let me wear it for a few minutes before you take it off."

"Deal."

Oh yeah, he could get used to this.

Chapter Twenty-One

The next morning, Penn woke up to sounds he didn't recognize. For one second, he was alarmed. He shot up, then glanced around the bedroom, finding touches of Gia everywhere. There were her slippers near the bed, her necklaces and earrings on the dresser, her books on the nightstand. Oh yeah, he wasn't living alone. Normally, he was a total grump when he woke up, so he reminded himself that he was here to impress Gia. She had to see what a great partner he'd be and that their marriage was a good investment.

He threw on some pants and found her in the kitchen, cooking something in a pan. She wore a red, green and white apron that read Bacia il Cuoco. He knew enough Italian to know what it meant and was happy to oblige. He came up behind her, wrapped his arms around her waist and kissed the cook.

"Good morning. The coffee is on the table. I thought you might be grumpy, so I didn't want to bother you too early."

"I'm not *always* grumpy." He rubbed his eyes. "Particularly when I have a great night."

He refused to admit he didn't eat breakfast. She'd obviously gone to the trouble of cooking for him too, not just for herself. Besides, having breakfast together was a good way to start the day, according to Hayes, resident relationship expert.

"What do you usually do on a Saturday morning?" She spooned some eggs onto a plate and handed it to him.

He worked, but that probably wouldn't go over well. If he was in this to win it, the marriage had to take priority.

"Usually I go for a run, then I…try to, you know, relax."

Okay, he was stretching the truth to what he wanted it to be. He *needed* to work less. Everyone told him the same thing. His mother, his brother. Ex-girlfriends. Even Madeline had mentioned it once, griping a little that he didn't have as much time to help them track down their missing brother. Penn tended to throw money at those problems. But if he wanted his marriage to Gia to be a success, and he did, he would put in the effort.

"Oh, same here," Gia said, taking a bite of eggs. "Except the running."

They ate breakfast together, then he helped her clean up. He changed for his run and before he left he found her looking through the closet.

"Back in a bit!" he called out, then headed down the elevator.

The doors opened on the fourth floor on the way down and his mother got on.

"Penn!" She reached to hug him.

Now that almost all his siblings were in Emerald Ridge, it took skill to avoid his relatives.

"Hey." He returned the hug. "Just going for my run."

"I'm sure you already know this, but Gia has moved into the building!" his mother gushed.

"Yeah, um, I heard that. She told me."

His mother put her palm up in a stop motion. "Now, I want you to calm down."

"*Calm down?* Why? What's going on now?"

"You probably think she's moving in so she can keep an

eye on you, monitor your comings and goings. Make sure you're not cheating on her."

He blinked. "Until you mentioned it, the idea hadn't even occurred to me."

"Of course, I know you're nothing like your father, may he rest in peace. But you can probably imagine some women are going to wonder about you. Particularly since you've never been married."

"Jesus, no, I'd never considered this. But thanks, Mom, for letting me know what people think," Penn muttered, raking a hand through his hair.

"They're wrong, of course, and you'll prove it to them. Just as soon as this whole inheritance mess is ironed out, we can all move on with our lives and put all the painful chapters behind us."

"Mom—" He realized one of those "painful chapters" was her own affair. He didn't want her to feel guilty, not anymore.

They both understood why she'd felt neglected by Archibald. He didn't want to make excuses for bad behavior but she needed to stop berating herself over it. At least now she could let go of the fear that Hayes was the other man's biological son, and not Archibald's. Taffy's stunt a few weeks ago to have all of their DNA tested had proven without a doubt he was Archibald's son, and thank God for that.

She waved her hand dismissively. "I wanted the DNA testing for years so I could be certain of what I suspected to be true. Now I have peace of mind."

Mom definitely found a way to see the glass half-full. The way she'd moved on inspired him. Maybe someday he could do the same, find a way to forgive the father he'd loved. The elevator doors swished open on the lobby floor and Penn waved to his mother as he took off down Main Street. He jogged past the storefronts. On the way back, he stopped inside Emerald Ridge Bakery to get pastries. He thought Gia would like the almond chocolate ones and grabbed a dozen.

"I'm back!" he yelled when he returned.

He set the pink box down and headed for the shower, tearing off his sweaty T-shirt with one hand as he strode down the hallway. As he stepped into the bedroom, he saw Gia sitting cross-legged on the bed—quickly closing her laptop as he walked in. Hmm. He wondered about it but decided to let it go. She deserved her privacy.

"How'd it go?" she asked.

"The run? Well, there's not much to say. It was fairly tame. I put one leg in front of the other, then repeat. You know how it goes."

"Okay, smartass." She stuck out her tongue.

"I did stop in and get pastries for us on my way back." He came closer and caught something out of the corner of his eye.

The closet door was open and his clothes were back. In fact, about half of the closet was filled with his clothes, and half with hers.

"You changed things." He scratched at his chin. "Why?"

"Because," she said. "This relationship is a two-way street and I don't want to take over and shove you out. I should just fit right in like a missing piece, not a brand-new puzzle."

Penn hated metaphors. He feared he didn't read enough fiction to truly understand them. "O-kay."

"What I meant is, I don't want to take over your entire closet. That's not fair. You need room in here, too."

"But I do have a whole other closet in the other bedroom." He plopped down on the bed next to her. "It's not like the penthouse is a small place."

"If it's *our* bedroom, then your clothes should be in here." She leaned against him, and damn it felt good to have her close.

He didn't hate being alone, or living alone, and never had. But this was better than he'd expected.

"I got to admit, it's Hayes who told me I should give you the entire closet. You know what, now that I think about it, maybe he was yanking my chain."

She snorted. "Uh-huh. Brothers. You have my sympathies because yes, I suspect he was teasing you. No woman alive expects the entire closet when she's living with her partner."

"Though I wouldn't be at all surprised if Hayes gave up his closet for Flora."

"You and he don't exactly dress the same," Gia remarked. "He's definitely low-key fashion in comparison to you."

"It's the nature of my business. If I showed up in jeans and a Stetson to my meetings, the board would probably ask for a psych eval."

Gia laughed. "Oh, what's not to love about a cowboy?"

"Not much, I hear." Penn remembered he'd been about to go in the shower and had been sitting here without a shirt for several minutes. "I was about to hop in the shower."

She kissed his shoulder. "I should join you. I haven't taken a shower yet either because I was—"

"Working?" He winked.

"Fine, you caught me. Just a few emails I responded to, no big deal. I guess maybe I work too much."

"Pot, meet kettle." He pointed to himself. "We really have to work on this, don't we?"

"I don't know about you, but I love my job. It could be better if Bella trusted me with the vines. She's very proprietary about the whole thing. Although I understand why, I would like to take more of a hands-on approach at the vineyard. Just because I'm good at selling doesn't mean I can't do other things. But it's the family business. That makes it hard to walk away from it some days." She lifted a shoulder. "And it's fun."

"When I get started on a new hotel, all the planning is like a drug that gets me high."

"It sounds like something we both need to work on. Bringing balance to our lives and not working all the time even if we love it. My sister Antonia has given me a few warnings that she worries I put too much of myself into the business."

"I like that we have the same problem."

He hesitated to mention what great partners they made, with compatible personalities, because he could sense Gia growing tired of it. A couple of times he'd seen her eyes glaze over at the word *partner*. Once, he caught her just shy of an eye roll. He realized she preferred the word *lover* but a lover was someone temporary and Gia was his wife. His… lifelong partner.

"C'mon, wife." He tugged her up by the elbow and led her into the en suite bathroom. "Let's take a shower together and conserve water. Later we can figure out how we're both going to learn to relax."

Chapter Twenty-Two

The shower was luxurious and Gia had never spent quite so much time taking one, but well… *Penn*. He turned a shower into a production for all the senses, the talented man.

"That was certainly…relaxing," Gia said, toweling off her hair.

"If that's relaxing, sign me up every day. I could get used to having a shower like this." Wrapped in a towel low on his lean hips, Penn slid her an easy smile. "But I'd need to schedule more time into my morning routine."

He was rather meticulous about his self-care, also very similar to Gia. They really were two of a kind. And even though they should be relaxing, they straightened up the apartment. Then Penn sat and picked up a book. Gia took a seat next to him and tried to read her latest thriller but read the same sentence three times. She could almost hear her laptop calling out to her, the ideas of new marketing angles coming to her rapid-fire. When one was too good to forget, she'd whip out her phone and make a note. Penn would slide her a look from under hooded eyes and then pick up his phone, too.

"Hey, want to go for a walk?"

Penn put down the book. "A walk where?"

"Just around. You're new in town—I owe you a tour."

Sitting still was driving her crazy. How did people *do* this?

Penn squinted. "Any place specific in mind?"

Gia honestly didn't know. She never went anywhere without a plan. When she took a walk, she had a destination. Otherwise, it would seem odd and possibly be a waste of time. *Time*, Papa Enzo told her once, was the one thing you couldn't buy despite having all the money in the world. But when she thought about the places she felt most relaxed, she never truly had a destination. Just being outdoors on the vineyard had been enough for years until at some point it turned into a purpose. Either she was talking about the year's harvest with Bella, assessing production levels, or making sure the tasting room looked cozy and inviting for customers.

Gone were the days of hanging a blanket between vines in her own private, imaginary world. Being an adult meant coloring *inside* the lines.

"Let's just figure it out as we go," Gia said. "The point is we'll be relaxing."

It was Penn's suggestion that they leave their phones behind to cut distractions and Gia agreed. She'd feel naked without her constant companion but she liked the challenge. They walked hand in hand down Main Street, exploring Emerald Ridge. She had to admit the place looked different than it did when she drove by mostly on her way to work. Even though she'd driven down these streets hundreds of times, she almost never walked.

"It's funny how much more you appreciate when you're not driving through." Gia pointed to a shop. "They totally changed the facade. How did I not notice?"

"You were too busy driving." Penn stopped in front of a flower shop and pulled her inside. "What's your favorite flower? I don't even know."

"I loved the roses you gave me, those were nice."

He waited a beat. "But?"

"My favorite flowers are yellow daffodils and you can only get those once a year."

"That makes them special," he murmured.

"But I also love bluebonnet season. I suppose every Texan does."

"Those are wildflowers. You can find them anywhere," Penn said.

"And your point is…?" She laughed.

Hand in hand, they walked through the shop admiring the arrangements. Gia thought of a real wedding, like the one she'd imagined as a child. She wouldn't share this with Penn but she'd had a dream wedding, and not surprisingly, it wasn't Lovers Lane Chapel in Las Vegas. If they stayed married, maybe they could have another, more official wedding. In her head, she started planning the flowers: baby's breath, unless that was too overdone. Maybe something yellow instead, if daffodils wouldn't work.

The door chimes rang out and a couple walked inside, arm in arm. It only took Gia a moment to recognize Madeline Fortune and her fiancé, Forrest Porter.

"Hey, you two!" Madeline called as they walked over. "What are you doing here?"

"Parasailing," Penn said with a smirk. "Why? What does it look like?"

"What a smartass!" Madeline said, thumping her brother's chest. "We have an appointment to pick the flowers for our wedding."

"I guess you do need flowers for a wedding," Penn mused, as if it had just occurred to him.

Suddenly Gia pictured the tacky bouquet of silk flowers she'd been holding on her wedding day. It hadn't seemed to matter much then—her focus had been entirely on the groom.

"I'm starting to remember how much you need for a wedding," Forrest said. "My first wedding wasn't a big deal."

"Well, that's what you get for asking an event planner to marry you!" Madeline leaned against his shoulder, beaming. "It's going to be the wedding of the year if I have anything to do with it."

"I'm sure it will be," Penn said.

"Oh! I see something has changed around here!" Madeline's bright eyes were pinned to Gia.

Only then did Gia realize she'd left the house without taking off the ring. She flushed, feeling the temperature in the shop warm to triple digits. "Oh, um…"

"Guess it's official." Penn took her hand and pulled it to his lips for a kiss. "She said yes."

Gia wondered how long it would be before everyone in the building knew. It would be an awful lot of people to disappoint if they wound up breaking up.

"I'm so happy!" Madeline hugged them both, and Forrest fist-bumped Penn. "I'll help you plan the wedding, no charge! Just be sure *not* to do it in June, which is my month."

"N-next June?" Gia stammered.

"It takes so much to plan a wedding and I've always wanted to be a June bride. Save the date!" Madeline took out her phone and made a note. "But I'll send official invites, of course."

"And don't be surprised if they're on gold parchment paper." Forrest winked.

Maybe sensing Gia's mounting panic at all this talk of June weddings, Penn squeezed her hand. "Well, we were just out for a Saturday afternoon stroll."

Madeline's blinked. "*Stroll?* Who strolls anymore?"

"We're trying to relax," Penn said. "We don't know how to *do* that."

"I miss relaxing," Forrest said with a deep sigh. "We have two toddler daughters and I haven't relaxed in years."

"Oh, pshaw!" Madeline elbowed him. "Relaxing is highly overrated."

Gia exchanged a look with Penn and she thought his gaze reflected what she was thinking: *Thank goodness someone else believes this.*

"So, Madeline," Penn said. "If you don't mind, would you keep our engagement quiet? For now, I mean. We just haven't told everyone yet and the families will be upset."

"Yes, please," Gia chimed in. "My family would disown me if they found out from someone else."

"Of course!" Madeline went hand to heart. "But what are you waiting for?"

"The right time," Gia said.

"You can count on me."

"More like you can count on *me*." Forrest held a finger to his lips. "I won't let her say a word."

"Thanks, guys. Really appreciate it." Penn clapped Forrest's shoulder. "Good luck with the flower choices."

"And you know who to call when you get ready for that engagement party." Madeline made a motion of putting an imaginary phone to her ear.

"Right." Penn pointed. "You'll be the first call we make."

Gia felt Penn's hand low on her back as they left the shop. Outside, in the bright pool of sunshine, she stared up at him and asked the question heavy on her mind.

"*Are* we going to have an engagement party?"

A party would be an announcement to everyone and she hadn't even decided yet.

Penn smiled. "Does that mean we're staying married?"

"I don't know. Ugh…this is getting so complicated." Gia

covered her face with her hands. “We can’t have an engagement party when we’re *already* married.”

“Who says? We get to make our own rules. It’s our marriage.”

They both glanced inside to see Madeline sweetly waving at them. Gia smiled and finger-waved back.

“Do you think she’ll keep quiet?”

Penn waved. “Let’s hope.”

Chapter Twenty-Three

Penn didn't think the start of his week and their new living arrangement could be going any better. He and Gia were finding their groove together, and as he'd anticipated, they were a couple perfectly suited to each other. If anyone were to look at them from the outside, they would conclude he and Gia had been together for years and were matched on some award-winning dating app boasting a 99.99 percent success rate. No one would ever guess they'd met and married the same night. It proved he could live with snap decisions. His instincts about people were still first-rate.

Their routine would change on Monday when they both resumed regular work hours, but for the past two days, they'd gone to bed together and got up at the same time. Penn tried not to even think about work, and to be honest, this had turned out to be easier than it ever had been before. When Gia gave him a wicked smile from across the room, dark wavy hair framing her face, he lost his train of thought.

On Sunday afternoon, the classic movie *An Affair to Remember* had just ended when Penn glanced at his watch and realized they'd have to leave soon to get to Hayes and Flora's ranch on time. They'd been invited to dinner, right after he told his brother that Gia had moved in with him and he gave her the entire closet. No doubt Hayes felt he had to see this kind of domestic bliss for himself.

As the credits rolled, Gia sniffed and reached for a tissue to dab at her eyes. “What did you think?”

She was a soft touch when it came to romantic movies. Like him. But this movie had irritated him. He wasn’t sure if he should say something about it to Gia. She’d wanted him to be honest, so in the end he went for it.

“I hated it.” Penn raked a hand through his hair. “Sorry.”

She blinked. “No, that’s fine. You can hate it. But what did you hate about it?”

He scratched his chin, remembering he’d forgotten to shave this morning. “Well…how do I put this? She’s guilty of having an emotional affair and finally confesses. Then she keeps the accident from Cary Grant assuming he won’t love her because she’s disabled. I guess… I didn’t find it romantic. In intimate relationships, people need to trust each other. And *talk* to each other. Think of how many problems could be avoided with a little bit of talking.”

Rather than be angry he’d just dissed one of her favorite movies, Gia smiled. “That’s what I think. My words almost exactly.”

“Yeah?”

Penn felt like he’d passed some kind of unwritten test. Being an overachiever all his life, little pleased him more than conquering a challenge.

“These are older movies and we need to remember that cultural attitudes have changed and improved in our generation. I view these old movies through that lens. When you know better, you do better.”

“Why is it one of your favorites?” He squeezed her tight. She’d been sitting close, in the crook of his arm, her legs curled under her on the couch.

“I just love the lush scenery, and mostly, Cary Grant. Yes,

it's a little melodramatic but the sacrificial love gets me every time." She laid her head on his chest.

He wrapped his arms around her and pulled her in even tighter. "I'm glad we think the same about this, too."

"Even the movie," she mumbled into his shirt.

"You wouldn't pull that sacrificial love stuff on me, would you?"

"Me? You mean if I'm in an accident and think you're not going to want to be with me anymore because I'm disfigured?"

"Yes, anything like that. You better never think I'd be better off without you. Because you're my wife any way you come. I won't ever leave you."

For a moment, she simply lifted her head to stare at him. She moved to frame his head between her hands. "You always seem to say the right things."

"Hmm, could it be because I'm the right man for you?"

"Yes, possibly."

She kissed him, long and deep, and heat coiled inside him.

"Oh!" She stopped suddenly and disentangled from his arms, standing up. "We're supposed to go to dinner with your brother today."

Still sitting, Penn reached for her arm and tugged her back in his lap. "We can be a little late..."

"No," she laughed, swatting his hand away. "I want to make a good impression on your brother."

"Not necessary. He already loves you."

"He doesn't even *know* me," Gia protested.

"I told him all about you."

She quirked a brow. "Really."

"Not *everything*. Remember, he's the one I first confided in about our quickie marriage."

"Did he think it was a good idea or a terrible one?" She got to her feet again and turned toward their bedroom.

"Hayes doesn't judge. He just wants me to be happy, whatever it takes." Penn followed her and pulled her back to him, stopping her forward momentum.

He wrapped his arms around her waist and nuzzled his face to her neck. "And it takes *you*."

Gia turned in his arms, and given her shimmering eyes, he could see the words had affected her.

She tugged on his hand and led him to the bedroom. "If we do this right, maybe we don't have to be late."

"I'm so nervous," Gia said a couple of hours later. "Do you think bringing wine is enough?"

"We weren't even asked to bring anything." He reached for her hand and squeezed it.

"I always like to bring something. I can't help it," Gia insisted, waving her hands in the air. "I'm Italian."

Penn chuckled as they both stood in front of the front door of the ranch-style home where Hayes and his fiancée lived. The homes in the neighborhood were new and lavish, each with plenty of land surrounding them. They were only renting this property, though, until they could find the ranch they wanted. One with the land and stables Hayes craved.

It occurred to Penn that several weddings were going to be happening around here, and funny how Penn beat them all to it. Not that this was a contest, but if it were, Penn would be winning. Just saying.

He'd barely knocked once when Hayes swung the door open then turned around to shout. "Hey! They're here, babe."

No sooner had they walked in the door than Mateo came toddling up behind his father, carrying a stuffed animal.

"Duck!" he said.

He was holding a teddy bear.

"Hiya, buddy. He's talking about me." Penn crouched to Mateo's height and pointed to himself. "Last time he saw me was the duck pond at the park, so you can see the connection."

"Nah, he calls everything a duck these days," Hayes muttered, picking up his son. "Yesterday he called me a duck."

"He meant dad," Penn said. "They both start with a *D*. Easy mistake."

"At least he's no longer gumming my Stetsons," Hayes chuckled, adjusting his hat.

"I brought some wine," Gia said, presenting the bottle. "It's a Burgundy Pinot Noir, one of our bestsellers."

"Enjoy," Penn said. "This is the wine we'll be serving at all my resorts since it's clearly the best."

"Hi." Flora joined them in the foyer, looking relaxed in jeans and a loose-fitting top. "Congratulations on your marriage."

"I thought you weren't going to say anything." Penn gave Hayes a censuring look.

"Hey, she's my other half!"

"Don't worry, I won't say anything." Flora held a finger to her mouth.

"Thank you," Gia said, handing her the wine. "We still have a few things to work out."

They all followed Flora through the hallway and out the back, onto a terra-cotta terrace where she'd set up a table under a wide umbrella. Although they still had some sunlight left in the late summer afternoon, there were lights strung from one end of the patio to the other.

"Oh, fairy lights. This is lovely," Gia murmured. "You have a beautiful home."

"Thank you," Flora said. "It's mostly land but I'm working to make it a home for us."

Dinner was a Tex-Mex extravaganza with steak nachos, chicken fajitas and queso with chips, which paired nicely with Gia's red wine.

"And no saffron in any of the dishes," Flora announced.

Gia seemed to slump a little in her seat beside him, so Penn put his arm around her shoulders. It was his fault he hadn't mentioned food allergies. Most people wouldn't think to ask. He never even mentioned it at restaurants since it was so rare the things he ordered contained saffron.

"How did you know?" Gia asked.

"Hayes told me when I asked him about any dietary restrictions," Flora said.

Gia slumped even farther and Penn lowered his hand to her thigh. "I should have asked."

"It's my fault," Penn declared. "I forgot to tell Gia and she made paella for me."

Flora's hand flew over her mouth. "Oh no!"

Hayes handed Mateo, in a highchair next to him, a piece of bread and he began to gum it into submission. "Easy mistake. Saffron is a bizarre ingredient for a food allergy. Leave it to Penn."

"Did you have a terrible reaction?" Flora asked, passing a plate of corn.

"Yes," Gia replied. "He had a rash which started to spread. I was scared to death!"

"She scares easily," Penn joked.

"Penn, that's a frightening thing, to watch someone you love hurting that way," Flora chided and gave Gia a sympathetic glance. "I might have done the same thing."

"Of course," Hayes said. "You would have called an ambulance. Mateo skinned his knee and she wanted to rush him to the emergency room."

Penn had a tough time but he restrained the laugh. This time Flora slumped a little in her chair.

"That was our first fight, actually," Gia said. "I was upset with him for not telling me, but mostly, I felt positively awful for what he went through."

"It's so hard when you love someone so completely." She gave her son the adoring look of a mother who would walk through fire for her child. "You can't stand them being hurt in any way. It's going to be even worse when you have a baby, Gia."

"Yeah, hopefully you won't have a baby also allergic to saffron because you know how hard it is to find baby food without *saffron* in it." Hayes rolled his eyes.

"Better to adopt and never risk passing on my horrible allergy," Penn said, rolling his eyes right back at Hayes.

"Oh, are you two thinking of adopting?" Flora asked, passing another piece of bread to Mateo.

He hadn't exactly planned on bringing up the subject, but now he had to roll with it. "Well, we just got married so we still have plenty of time. But in my opinion blood doesn't matter when it comes to children."

And when Gia smiled up at him with glistening eyes, Penn knew he'd said the right thing.

Chapter Twenty-Four

Gia enjoyed the dinner and conversation with Flora, who reminded Gia of her own sisters—self-possessed and confident in their skills as mothers. It must be so lovely to have a baby. A pang shot through her heart. She couldn't have the one thing that even money couldn't buy. *Fertility.* But it was a balm to her soul to know Penn didn't see her as lacking, even as he doted on his adorably sweet nephew—Hayes' mini-me—with the same eyes, hair color, straight nose and impish smile.

She helped Flora clear the table while the men entertained Mateo outside by tossing him a ball back and forth.

"I hope Hayes didn't speak out of turn but he did tell me that you two were married pretty unexpectedly in Las Vegas."

Flora was kind enough not to ask any questions.

"This time what happened in Vegas *didn't* stay in Vegas," Gia chuckled, handing Flora a plate. "But honestly, I don't regret it."

A warm and sweet feeling passed through her, knowing for the first time the truth of this. No matter what happened in the future between her and Penn, she'd always treasure and remember these days together.

"Sometimes the best things in life are surprises," Flora said. "I certainly didn't plan on Mateo, but he's the best thing to ever happen to me."

"I've heard that about children," Gia said, still unable to talk about her infertility despite the woman's kindness.

"Sometimes things just work out. I hope that's the case with you and Penn. You both seem like two of a kind."

Gia arched a brow. "How do you mean?"

This seemed to be something Penn kept emphasizing and drilling into her to make his case to stay married. But she still wasn't sure they were all *that* similar. After all, Penn had a logical way of looking at relationships while Gia thought love couldn't always be rational. You loved who you loved, even though if you stopped to analyze it, loving someone probably meant they complemented an unspoken part of you.

"You're both busy professionals, and yet now both ready to settle down. And honestly, you *look* so good together. Just… shiny and bright." Flora laughed. "I've always thought Penn looked like he stepped out of the pages of *GQ* magazine and now you…you're his perfect match. Plus, you two seem to really support each other. That's so important."

Gia wanted to believe it, and everything he said was almost exactly what she needed to hear from him. All except for… love. He'd never once told her he loved her. The lack of those words when everything else seemed too perfect had begun to feel like percussion out of step with the rest of the band. She tried to ignore it. They still had time. Several moments this weekend, she'd been about to tell him she loved him. Someone had to go first, and she didn't have any hang-ups about this. When he shared how he felt about *An Affair to Remember*, she'd almost told him right then and there. But she'd held back, and didn't understand what was stopping her other than fear. In his mind, they had a deal for a partnership, and if she mentioned love, he might want to walk away from it all.

"This weekend we've both tried to relax and stop working. We even left our phones behind and took a walk through town."

"A walk is good for the soul."

Gia nodded. "The problem, if you want to call it that, is we both love our work. Maybe we love it *too* much."

"It's important to find time for each other and make it a priority. When you have a family that becomes more essential than ever."

"Of course. I know you're right."

No need to tell Flora how difficult it might be to *have* a family. Everything Gia had heard about adoption indicated plenty of red tape and years of waiting for the opportunity. With all their money and resources, they'd at least look good on paper, but that didn't guarantee anything.

"Let's just leave these dishes and go join the guys." Flora threw the dish towel on the counter. "Life is too short and this mess will be here in the morning."

They stepped outside, to where the evening sun had crested and the crickets had begun to chirp all around them. Penn, who'd been literally sitting on the grass with Mateo, turned to her and met her gaze. His always perfectly coiffed hair was mussed the way it only was in the morning. A lock fell over one eye, giving him a positively boyish look. He smiled and Gia felt a swift and powerful tug to her heart. Her heart had a mind of its own and it told her she was in love with Penn Fortune.

No doubt about it, she was in trouble.

Later that night, back at Penn's penthouse suite, Gia slipped under the covers next to him. He opened his arms to pull her in close. She absolutely loved that he didn't mind cuddling and seemed to enjoy it as much as she did. Funny because he did not look like a cuddler.

"Not going to lie," she murmured, resting her head on his chest. "You looked good with Mateo. Like you were born to be a dad."

He played with her hair as he'd been doing every night, curling his fingers through it. "I don't know if anyone is born to be a dad. Look at my own father. He was blessed with plenty of children, but he obviously didn't know *how* to be a father. Biology doesn't make someone a dad. At some point, desire and ambition has to be part of it."

"You're right. I suppose what's instinctive to some isn't to everyone. I think *you'll* make a good father."

"I will be a very different kind of father. I'll be present and available which is something my own father rarely gave us. It seemed to come pretty instinctively to Hayes, too." He smoothed her hair down. "Do you worry I'm going to cheat on you? You mentioned this once before. Does that thought like…still come up?"

The words were alarming enough for her to lift her head from his chest and stare up at him. "Why would it? You said you'd be faithful to me if we stay married."

He shook his head. "Nothing for you to worry about. Just something someone said that has me worried."

"Worried? Why are you *worried*?"

"I've been a commitment-phobe vibe for most of my adulthood. Apparently my mother thinks because both of my parents cheated on each other, I think *everyone* does, which is why I've never settled down before. Of course, that's not at all why. First, I've never cheated on a girlfriend. Yeah, it's been tough to find someone but it's not like I haven't tried. But she also doesn't realize I'm *already* married. I'm obviously not allergic to commitment."

Not allergic to commitment, but perhaps a little leery of

love, it would seem. But Gia didn't want to be negative in this near-perfect moment.

"I don't see you that way at all. You're serious about marriage. So am I."

"Point is, I don't want *you* to think that about me. Believe me, sweetheart, I'm all in with us. One hundred percent."

Reassured—at least for now—Gia laid her head back on his chest. "I believe you. You make it easy."

"I hope so because I don't want you to have any doubts."

There was only one and she had a decision to make.

I love you, I love you, I love you, Gia wanted to say. But how would he react if she told him now? Would he awkwardly thank her for loving him, or confess he'd fallen for her, too? Sooner or later, she would have to bring up the subject.

But not tonight.

"Next Sunday, I'd like you to come to Sunday dinner with *my* family."

He tugged on a lock of her hair. "Really? You're ready to tell them about us?"

"I think I just might be. It's time."

"Then I'll be there."

Chapter Twenty-Five

The week passed smoothly, with Gia going in to the office each day and Penn working from home. But every night they'd have dinner together and watch a movie or play a board game before bedtime. That was always the best part, going to bed together, waking up together. Gia was living a dream in some ways, but it occurred to her she'd been misleading Penn—letting him believe this loveless arrangement he'd proposed would work.

But that was because it didn't *feel* loveless to her.

Penn was tender, affectionate and loving, not simply interested in sexy times. Even though, of course he was extremely interested, as was she. But they had a solid foundation. Maybe...she'd halfway convinced herself to settle for this arrangement because it didn't *feel* like settling. It felt like... everything.

But the one-sided nature of one person in love wasn't fair. In her case, she'd failed to keep this to a partnership. It was so much more than that to her. She'd fallen head over heels in love with her husband.

Later that morning, she reminded Penn about Sunday dinner at her family mansion.

"Oh, shit. I forgot about that!" Penn raked a hand through his messy morning hair.

She didn't know whether she believed him, or if he was making up an excuse not to go.

"If we're going to stay married, Penn, we need to tell my family together. That's the deal."

"I know, babe. I know." He held her close, pressed her into his arms. "And I want to, but I can't today."

"Is it your family?"

She'd already seen the way discussion of the inheritance and anything regarding Oliver sent him to a dark place.

He wouldn't meet her eyes, and his body caved in a little, as if guilt had pressed down in one sudden swoop.

"You won't like this, but I have a business meeting over Zoom. It's a possible hotel deal I've been trying to nail down in Australia for months. It's already Monday there."

This was true, so she could hardly blame the timing. It technically violated their no-work-on-the-weekend agreement but through no fault of his own.

"I guess you get a pass, then. Next time we'll tell them together."

Though disappointed, she didn't want to start this marriage off by being so stringent about rules. There might come a time when she had to meet a client on a weekend. She'd certainly had to in the past.

"Thank you, babe. Thank you." He pressed his forehead to hers and kissed her. "I will make it up to you."

When Gia arrived, everyone was already sitting. Mama and Papa Enzo sat on opposite ends of the large farmhouse-style family table that seated twelve. Bella and her kids were here, along with Leo, his wife, Poppy, and their little boy, Joey. Also present were Antonia and her husband, Roth Fortune, with their one-year-old daughter, Georgie.

"Ah! There she is." Papa Enzo held his arms out in welcome. "The missing one."

Gia gave him a hug first, then went around the table. "Sorry I'm late."

She told herself maybe it was for the best that Penn hadn't come to dinner tonight to officially meet her family. If time permitted, she'd bring it up to her sisters. She'd tell them slowly, confiding everything. Then, her sisters would help break the news to Mama in the best way. They were staying married. The annulment papers were still in her bag, practically forgotten. She hadn't signed them, not after Penn asked her to move in with him. This was huge progress, and over the past week, they'd been getting along so well. It gave her hope that he'd turned a corner and was open to love.

"How've you been, sis?" Leo elbowed her. "Haven't seen much of you lately since that trip to Vegas."

"Why did you miss your flight, anyway?" Antonia asked, adjusting Georgie into her high chair.

"Oh, um, yeah. The weather was bad and they rescheduled me."

Gia hated lying to her family but telling them she'd overslept and missed her flight because she was too busy nursing a hangover after getting married might not go over well at this point. Baby steps. First, she had to tell her sisters privately. They'd understand the whole hot guy thing better than Mama or Papa Enzo would. In fact, they should probably *never* tell Papa.

Mama asked Leo to say the blessing and afterwards they passed around plates of risotto, crusty garlic bread and lasagna.

After a few minutes, Bella stood. "I've paired a new vino for tonight. It's something new and I'd like your opinion."

Leo immediately approved, followed by everyone else. Gia

thought it reminded her far too much of the cabernet that went down so easily she wound up drunk. She decided to have one glass tonight and not an ounce more.

"You never told us," Bella said. "Which wine did Penn Fortune like best?"

"Penn *Fortune*?" Roth asked from next to Antonia. Roth was one of the Fortunes from another branch, a distant cousin to Penn.

"He's come to Emerald Ridge to deal with his father's will," Gia explained. "And while I was in Vegas, I hit him up to carry Leonetti wines in all of his hotels. He agreed. Oh, and his favorite wine was the cabernet sauvignon."

"That whole family thing sure sounds like a mess." Leo changed the subject and served his son another helping of lasagna. "Imagine finding out that your father had two other families."

Everyone grumbled and Mama crossed herself.

"And a third brother they may have just located," Gia added. "Remember the man who visited us here not long ago? Oliver Webb? Well, believe it or not, *he's* their missing heir."

"That nice young fella?" Mama said. "The poor man grew up without a father, didn't even know much about his mother's past."

"To be honest, this whole scandal has reflected poorly on that side of the family." Roth shook his head. "I wouldn't want to be in their position. It's a lot to live down."

"Exactly," Poppy said.

Gia's sympathy for Penn renewed, remembering how he'd joked that she should be the one wary to link her family lineage to his. There was a sense of shame in him, even if he hadn't been the one to cause his family such pain. Gia could sense he expected a great deal from the people he loved. And the father he'd once loved had disappointed him in ways that could hardly be described.

After their amazing dinner, followed by Mama's special tiramisu for dessert, Gia helped clear the table. The kids, let loose outside, chased each other as the summer sun began its slow dip down the horizon. Tonight was the first official day of summer, the longest day of the year.

"I've been meaning to tell you." Mama stood at the sink rinsing a plate. "My friend Elena has a son who'd would be perfect for you. He's a *doctor*."

Gia snorted. "What makes you think a doctor would be perfect for me?"

"Well, he's wealthy and you won't have to worry like with that awful Marco." Mama shook her head, her lips pinched in disgust.

This seemed as good a time as any to start the process with her mother. "Actually, I'm…seeing someone new and it's becoming serious."

She brightened. "Yes? Who is he? Do I know him?"

"It's…actually, it's Penn. Penn Fortune."

Mama clapped a hand over her mouth, then lowered it. "Mio dio! And we were gossiping about his family at dinner."

"It's okay, he'd be the first to admit how crazy it all is." Gia rinsed a plate and stacked it in the dishwasher. "He's not proud of it."

Just then Bella walked in. "What did I miss?"

"Gia is dating Penn Fortune!" Mama clapped her hands together. "And it's serious!"

Bella squealed. "Why didn't you tell me?"

"Because you're going to make a big thing out of this." Gia turned and put both hands on her hips. "It's no big deal."

"No big deal? *No big deal*, she says!" Bella leaned out the kitchen doorframe into the family room and cupped her hands over her mouth. “Antonia! 911!”

“Say it loud enough so people in Dallas can hear you.” Gia scowled. “Not *everyone* has to know my business.”

Antonia almost skidded to a stop inside the kitchen. “Is someone hurt?”

“No, but any minute now…” Gia said, scowling in Bella’s direction.

“Gia is dating the biggest catch in town!” Bella exclaimed. “Penn *Fortune*!”

“What? Are you serious?” Antonia said. “*Another* Fortune? Well, he can’t be better than mine.”

“Or mine,” Leo said, appearing with Poppy after hearing the commotion, his arm draped over his wife’s shoulders.

“All I asked you to do was get him to sell our wines in his hotels.” Her brother smirked, characteristically saying exactly what Gia thought he would. “You didn’t have to date the guy.”

Poppy glanced up at him adoringly. “They must have really hit it off, and it’s all thanks to you!”

“Be sure to put me in your will and that will be thanks enough. You’re welcome.” Leo kissed his wife on the lips. “I’m going to go see what the kids are doing.”

“Gia, tell us all about him.” Poppy demanded, coming up to her. “Penn’s from Houston, so I’ve never even met him though we’re distantly related.”

“I’ll have to introduce you,” Gia said. “And Roth, too. I actually asked him to dinner tonight, but it didn’t work out.”

“He sounds like he’s got a lot going on with all those family issues,” Antonia remarked.

“Yes,” Gia said. “They hired a PI to find the missing brother. He’s here in Emerald Ridge now.”

“Hope that works itself out,” Poppy said. “It’s great Penn was able to locate the brother.”

"His name is Oliver Webb, the man that came around here a few months ago asking questions about his mother," Gia said. "I'm so glad I remembered him."

"Poor man." Mama wrung her hands together. "He didn't even know his own father. Tragic."

"When will we meet Penn?" Antonia asked.

"I'm sure you'll meet him soon."

Although being here tonight and watching her siblings who were so obviously in love, Gia didn't know if she could do this anymore. She'd need *all* of him, not just whenever he felt like he wanted to play husband. He had a mercurial temperament at times and she could handle that. What she couldn't handle was being married to someone who refused to fall in love with her.

"Mommy, where's the candy?" Bella's son carried Gia's bag into the kitchen with him. "I ate my dinner."

"That's not my purse, sweetie." Bella moved to take it from him, but it fell out of her son's hands, spilling some of the contents on the terra-cotta floor.

Though Gia tried to beat Bella to her purse, she couldn't get there in time.

"That's *my* bag." Gia reached for the annulment papers too late.

Bella held them up, eyes wide. "What's this?"

"None of your business, that's what!" She ripped them out of Bella's hands, barely caring about the pained look on her sister's face.

Privacy had always been hard-won in the Leonetti household.

"Gia," Mama scolded. "Don't talk to your sister like that."

"I'm sorry, it's just this is nobody's business." Gia tucked the papers back into her purse.

Gia caught Bella and her mother exchange a significant look.

"You keep secrets from *your family*?" Mama clutched her heart.

"It's not a secret. This…this is complicated." Gia didn't know how she'd get out of this one. She had to think fast.

"They're *annulment* papers," Bella said in an accusing tone. "Made out to Gia and Penn Fortune."

Mama gasped and crossed herself. "Dio mio."

"Bella! You held my secret for ten lousy seconds!" Gia shook a finger at her. "That must be a record, your personal best."

"Mommy!" The boy pulled on Bella. "I want my candy!"

Bella bent to talk to her son. "In a minute, baby."

"Nooo!" he howled.

"I'm insulted." Antonia crossed her arms. "This is big news. And I thought we were close."

"Let me see those papers!" Mama reached for Gia's bag.

"No!" Gia pulled her purse away. "It's just a form I downloaded."

"And then *filled out*?" Bella said, over the sound of her son's whines. "It was filled out, Mama!"

"It's not completely filled out!" Gia yelled.

"Dio mio!" Mama cried again.

Suddenly, Roth appeared in the doorway. "What the hell is going on in here?"

Bella walked over to Roth. "Do me a favor? Please take him to my purse and give him the candy I promised him earlier."

Roth narrowed his eyes, picked the boy up and carried him out of the kitchen.

Then she turned to Gia, hands on hips. "Let's talk about this."

Gia covered her face with her hands. "It's so embarrassing."

"What happened?" Antonia came close, putting her arm around Gia. "Maybe we can help."

"I doubt that." Gia gestured toward the dining area where Papa sat near the window, watching the children play outside. "And I don't want Papa Enzo to hear any of this."

"Let's go in my room." Mama turned to lead them to her bedroom on the first floor and it was far enough in the back of the house that Papa couldn't hear. "Papa, we'll be right back."

He raised a hand, still facing the window, where Bella's children were engaged in a game of tag outside. "Si."

All four women walked into Mama's bedroom, where she still had the same mahogany four-poster bed she'd slept in with her husband for decades. The roomed smell liked roses, and the St. Mary's candle Mama regularly burned.

Mama shut the door. "Now, what is this annulment?"

"Yeah, don't you have to be married to have one of those?" Bella plopped down on the edge of the bed.

Antonia gave Bella an "are you stupid" look. "*Why yes*, you do."

"When did you have time to get married?" Bella prodded. "It's only been a week since you went to Vegas and—"

Dead silence as Antonia and Bella stared at each other, eyes wide, then turned to Gia when understanding hit them.

"Are you kidding me?" They both spoke at once.

"What?" Mama was obviously still confused, not putting the elements together as quickly, though give her five, four, three…

"Mio dio, did *Elvis* marry you?"

"No, an Elvis impersonator did not marry me." Gia crossed her arms. "It was a lovely man."

"But it sure wasn't a church wedding." Bella bit her lower lip, like she was holding back a laugh.

Antonia put her hands on Mama's shoulders. "Why don't you go check on Papa?"

"But—" the older woman began.

"I think I heard him cough." Antonia gently pushed Mama to the door, hand on her back. "Don't worry, Bella and I will fix this."

"You will?" Her eyes went wildly between all three of her daughters, scanning and computing. She gestured between them. "And you three won't fight?"

Gia saw Bella do her best imitation of an angel. "When do we *ever*?"

Antonia slowly closed the door and turned to Gia. "Now, you can spill everything and you don't have to hold back for Mama's sake. Tell us the raw, unvarnished truth."

Bella waved at the air between them. "This is a nonjudgement space."

Gia sighed and slowly slumped to the bed where she sat. "Fine."

And then she told them everything.

Chapter Twenty-Six

"I *knew* it!" Bella snapped her fingers and began to pace the room. "It's my wine. Nobody can resist the flavor. I'm a certified genius. I think we need to rebrand that particular wine. A new campaign! How about Amore?"

"It is a great wine," Gia agreed. "And a little dangerous if you happen to be in Vegas vibing with an extremely hot guy and a chapel right downstairs."

"We'll use a silly label. *Warning: Choose wisely and drink with caution, you might fall in love!*" Bella, on a roll, spun like a top.

Antonia glared at their oldest sister. "Shame on you. We have bigger problems than our next marketing campaign!"

"Oh, yeah." Bella stopped spinning. "I'm so sorry, that's *awful*. You're secretly married to the most eligible bachelor in town. I've seen the guy and my heart bleeds for you."

"Bella," Antonia spoke between clenched teeth. "This is complicated, as Gia said. First, there's the fact Mama always pictured her youngest in a church wedding and this Vegas sham is not *any* parent's dream."

"Which is why I didn't want you all to blab to Mama! I knew she'd be disappointed."

"Of course she is. Second, well, there's the whole annulment thing. I'm going to guess you're both not planning to *stay* married, which is why you haven't told us."

"Actually," Gia said, tracing the rose pattern on her mother's bedspread. "He wants to stay married."

"Say what?" Antonia's neck swiveled back.

Bella snapped her fingers. "He wants to stay married because of course he does. Look at our little sister. She's *gorgeous*! I'm not surprised he fell in love at first sight. I mean, I've heard of this kind of thing happening but never knew anyone personally."

"And you still *don't* know anyone." Gia sighed sadly. "He doesn't love me."

"Ah," Antonia said. "That's what these annulment papers are about. You won't stay married if he doesn't love you."

"That makes total sense." Bella nodded. "I divorced my husband for similar reasons."

"The thing is, he *behaves* like a man in love. All the things he does for me and the way he treats me…and—" Gia reached inside her bag for the ring box. She slipped the wedding ring on her finger. "He wanted me to have this and said I could keep it even if we don't stay married."

Both of her sisters inspected the beautiful ring, and going by their smiles, they approved.

"That's probably seven carats," Antonia said. "It's truly beautiful."

"What you haven't said is whether *you* love him," Bella pointed out. "Doesn't that matter at all?"

"I'm falling in love with him. Maybe I'm already there." Gia held her wedding band up to the light. "It's not about the ring. I told him I can't have children, and he doesn't care. Oh, he wants kids, that's the main reason he wants to stay married. But he said we can adopt and he's fine with that."

"Wow, okay," Bella said. "So, he must love you, right?"

"He hasn't said that. He likes what we have, a partnership. I thought I could get him to fall in love with me. I just need a little time…"

"How do you know he's not falling for you?" Antonia asked.

"I don't know for sure. Even I haven't told him that I love him. We just don't say the words. And it's the way he keeps talking about a loveless marriage, and a 'true' partnership." Gia held up air quotes. "But lately, things have been so good. I…moved in with him—*temporarily*—so we can give the marriage an honest try. He couldn't come tonight due to a meeting but we were going to tell you all tonight."

"So, that means you're staying married to him?" Bella sounded hopeful to Gia.

"I want to, but I need him to believe in love. Sometimes I have to think that if he's got such preconceived notions about marriage, maybe this is a battle I can't win." Gia's lower lip trembled and she felt dangerously close to real tears.

"But how long are you supposed to stay in a loveless marriage?" Bella asked.

"Exactly." Antonia lowered her head like she was thinking this over. "I agree. You can't stay in a marriage like that. And right now, you're in limbo. You have to know exactly how he feels."

"But…isn't that pushing things?" A tear slipped down Gia's cheek and she brushed it away. "We might be married, but we're still getting to know each other."

Antonia hugged Gia. "Oh, honey. I know you too well to think you'd ever be happy in a marriage where your husband isn't madly in love with you. You're a romantic, not a pragmatist."

"I am." Gia had to acknowledge this, and yes, it had been bothering her not to know whether Penn could at least be open to loving her someday. Preferably soon.

"If you think about it, there's a reason those papers are still in your bag," Bella said. "You still have doubts."

"No, I don't," Gia protested. "I don't clean out my purse that often."

Both sisters exchanged glances.

"Look, here's what you have to do," Antonia said.

Her big sister then suggested a step-by-step plan that should get her the answers she craved.

If nothing else, Gia would have resolution once and for all and be able to move forward.

Gia came back from dinner with leftovers for Penn. When she walked inside the apartment, he was sitting on the couch in front of his laptop but stood up and closed the distance between them. He drew her into his arms, lifted her hand and brought the ring up to his lips, brushing a kiss across her knuckles.

"I missed you. How did it go?"

"I missed you too." She didn't know how to answer his question since it hadn't gone well at all. "Mama sent some leftovers."

"Thanks, babe." He took the cartons. "I haven't eaten all day. The meeting went on and on."

She followed him into the kitchen, getting plates and silverware for him and setting them down.

He opened the carton of lasagna and made an approving sound. "Did you tell your family about us?"

They'd agreed that she would pave the way by telling her family they were dating and serious about each other, which she'd done.

"Yes, but…it got very complicated." She worried a fingernail between her teeth, a habit she'd let go of when she was a teenager. It was back in spades.

"Yeah? How so?" Penn spooned some of the lasagna on to a plate and popped it in the microwave.

"Well… I'm sorry, Penn, but they know. My sisters found out because they're snoops and tattletales!" Great, now she *sounded* like a teenager, too.

Penn chuckled. "It's okay. It would have happened sooner or later, right? I just wish I could have been there with you. Did they take it well?"

"Not at all, because…they found the annulment papers in my bag."

"*What* annulment papers?" He squinted.

That's right, she'd never told him, because after she'd printed and started to fill them out, everything had taken a turn for the better. She'd met his mother. Then they'd moved in together and had been getting along like honeymooners. And yes, she'd wanted to forget the papers. Maybe, however, as Antonia had said, there was a reason they were still in her bag. She had to be sure and there was only one real way to do this.

"It's a long story, but my bag fell open and out came the papers. Bella grabbed them and she told my mother. That's how they found out we were married—in Las Vegas."

Penn groaned and palmed his face.

"No one is upset with you," Gia assured him. "We're both equally to blame and the Leonettis are an equal-opportunity family."

"What I don't understand is what the annulment papers were doing in your bag." He gazed at her with a look equal parts frustration and something like pain. "Is that why you asked for my birth date?"

"Yes," she said with no small amount of guilt. "It was painful to realize I didn't even know my husband's birthday. We don't know each other at all in so many ways."

"We can learn about each other and that's what we've been doing. I thought we… I thought things were going well."

"They are, but I'd printed them before. In the early days, you know. Last week."

Penn's jaw tightened to granite. "So, you've been sleeping next to me every night, making me think we stood a chance, all while those papers were in your *bag*? Why didn't you get rid of them?"

"I—I was going to do that."

"Well, here, let me help you." He stalked to her purse, every step pounding with frustration, and handed it to her. "I want to watch you tear them up in front of me."

This wasn't going well. She hadn't expected him to be so angry. Then again, she'd also kept the fact that she'd downloaded the papers from him. This was all because she had hoped she wouldn't need them, but now she saw his side of it. It must feel like a betrayal to have already lost her faith in this working.

"I would love to tear these up, but one of the things I've learned is my new husband doesn't believe in love. You're jaded and don't have a lot of faith in your ability to love." Her voice broke.

"Can you blame me? My family is like a circus show."

"Yes, but you're not your father," she whispered. "You don't ever have to make the choices he did."

He released a ragged breath, shoulders stiffening. "And I won't but that doesn't change facts. Love doesn't work because it won't last, even if the people involved mean well."

"It's a risk but one worth taking and that's where we're too different. Anyway, it's too late for me." She raised her head to meet his eyes, voice trembling. *"I am already in love with you, Penn."*

Saying the words out loud, she realized how true they

were. And it hurt, like a knife slicing through her heart, to see the look on his face as she spoke. It was nothing less than paralyzing fear.

"Gia—"

"Don't." She put a finger to his lips. "I love you because of who you are. Your strength, your kindness, your tenderness, your *ability* to love."

"But I can't—I don't want to ruin what we have here between us. A true partnership and mutual respect. Those are the things that last in a marriage. We can go the distance."

"You're not wrong, and I understand those are the building blocks of a marriage so when you get to tough times, you'll make it to the other side. But I need more than that. Maybe I'm foolish...but I—I need your heart." She took a deep breath and followed Antonia's advice. "If you can tell me you love me, you be the one to rip up those papers."

"I do love you, Gia. There's such a thing called platonic love. Are you telling me you've never felt that way before about someone? Love but without the ups and downs of being *in love*? It's completely logical and far less painful."

This was exasperating—not going entirely to plan. Gia had hoped this would be the moment Penn finally woke up and *realized* he was in love with her, a turning point for them both.

Apparently not.

"You couldn't make love to me the way you do and not return my feelings. You're passionate. Everything you do—everything you've shown me—means you must be falling in love, too."

"But that's not what I want!" For the first time, he raised his voice. "Damn, Gia, *you're* what I want. This marriage and the way we are together. Having children, living a good life. I can give you all that. I'll give you more than any other man ever will." He shoved a hand through his hair, his control slipping. "You shouldn't get hung up on this one little thing. I'm not the *type* of man to fall in love, and that shouldn't be a deal-breaker."

"It is for me. I'll leave these with you." Her movements shaky, she pulled the papers out and handed them to him. "They need your signature anyway."

Penn dropped them on the couch. "That's it? You're just going to end our *marriage*?"

"I'm sorry." She slipped off her ring and quietly set it on the coffee table.

Gia held back tears because he'd only want to comfort her. Like a *friend.* Which was all he wanted to be. Well, she had lots of friends, and also plenty of family. She wanted a lover and not just a partner, but someone who would give her his whole heart. If it wasn't him, she'd have to let him go.

"I'll come back to get my stuff later." Gia walked toward the door, her heart shattering more with every step.

"Gia, sweetheart, don't do this." Penn followed her to the door. "We *have* something here."

"I know we do, but it's not complete." She turned to caress his jawline one last time, listening to the prickle of beard stubble scrape against her fingernails. "I'm going to miss you. You'll always be my first. I wanted it to be you and me, *forever*, but falling in love can't be forced. A heart has to be open first. I think you'll get there, someday, in your own time. At least I hope so—for your sake. Even if it means it won't be me."

Gia turned, opening the door slowly, hoping any minute he'd stop her, pull her into his arms and admit he loved her. But when that moment didn't come, she took the elevator downstairs, and once outside, stepped into the car that would take her home.

Chapter Twenty-Seven

As a rule, Penn hated Mondays on principle. Now he hated them based on facts. Mondays would forever be the day after his wife asked him for an annulment—just as he was getting used to the word *wife*. This Monday, he woke up alone, the wedding ring he'd given her on the table where she'd left it. Gia was completely illogical, of course, but he saw no way left to convince her. He'd pulled out all the stops, showing rather than simply telling her what a great husband he could be. But *she* chose to fixate on the fact he didn't believe in love the same way she did. It was patently unfair.

He loved her like a member of his own family—the people he *loved*, that is. With their numbers growing, he couldn't speak for everyone.

He loved his mother, Hayes, Flora and Mateo. He'd even come to love his half sisters. Certainly, he'd loved his father… and look where *that* got him. It got him a half brother who deeply resented the rest of his siblings for everything they'd been given and he had not. It got him a piece of land where they might discover more about their family, but said piece of land was tied to the brother who didn't want anything to do with them. *Good work, Dad.*

The rest of the morning, he tried to get some work done, but his focus was nonexistent. His eyes kept drifting to the annulment papers, which he silently hoped would just disappear. Of course, that wasn't going to happen, and he knew he should sign them. Because that was what she wanted...even though *he* still didn't want this. Maybe if he hung on a few more days, she'd change her mind, but deep down he understood she was right. It wasn't fair to force her to accept the marriage on his terms.

The next two days passed in something closely resembling a living hell as Penn negotiated and closed deals, hit the gym and thought endlessly about Gia. He relived the first moment he'd laid eyes on her in his Vegas office—the spark that flickered in him at her smile—knowing somehow nothing would ever be the same again. He remembered the first flight where he'd had to land in a monsoon. She was nothing like what he'd expected of a beautiful and privileged woman: down to earth, family-oriented, sexy, passionate and tender.

His dream girl.

It had been a short time and she'd changed him—but not for the better. He'd gone from a happy-go-lucky, occasionally grumpy man dealing with a profitable business to a permanently grumpy man dealing with a profitable business. Because now, for the first in his life, he understood what he was missing out on.

Feeling restless and out of sorts, he dropped by Hayes and Flora's ranch after work. No one but Mateo could put a smile on Penn's face now. He found father and son outside on the rolling green hills of the Rodriguezes' property.

Penn had hoped to raise his children on Leonetti land. The gardens there were lush and green, and he could almost see his children playing the games he and Hayes had as children. He'd imagined a girl and a boy, however, one for him and one for Gia. Now he had no kids in mind for the foreseeable future. A burning disappointment made him feel it wasn't worth it. Maybe he'd simply be Uncle Penn and that should be enough. There was no point in having children with a woman who would always feel inferior to Gia in his mind.

"Hey, there." Penn walked up to his brother. "Flora said you'd be out here."

Mateo turned, a huge grin on his face. "Duck!"

A bird that had just alighted on the ground flew away with a branch.

"Well, it's easier to say than bird," Penn chuckled. "And it's another animal, so he's not wrong."

"Exactly, he gets it," Hayes said. "But it's *bird*, buddy."

Mateo smiled shyly and buried his face in his father's neck. "Duck."

"Now he's just messing with you," Penn said, ruffling his nephew's hair. "Definitely *your* son."

Hayes snorted. "Hey, Flora wants to have everyone over to the house this week. The sisters and their husbands—and Oliver."

"What's the occasion?"

His brother shrugged. "Her misguided effort to bring us all together as a family. But hey, it *could* work."

"Sure, not much else we can do but wait."

"If anyone can bring this blended family together, Flora can."

Penn thought of someone else who would have been able to do that, too, but now Gia was out of the picture.

"Your lovely secret wife is also invited, of course. Her charms might work on Oliver in case Flora's fail."

"She won't be coming, as she's not going to be my wife much longer." Jaw tightening, Penn stuck his hands in the pockets of his jeans.

"Uh-oh. She didn't go with the idea of a loveless marriage?"

"Nope," Penn said. "She claims I must love her because

of the way I take care of her. And I do love her, but not in the way she wants. She's like family to me, someone I care about deeply. I want her to be my wife, and I'd think that should mean something."

Hayes sighed and put Mateo down, who toddled away toward the fence line. The two of them followed close behind.

"There's something I didn't mention to you about that day at the park when you watched the dude flirting with Gia," his brother said. "Remember when I was surprised you were that possessive?"

"Because she's my *wife*," Penn growled.

"Right," Hayes said. "And I didn't know that at the time. But. Here's the thing—if 'wife' was just a noun, or a title you've given her, would it seriously piss you off that much?"

"I was sleeping with her, too."

"Sure, yeah. You were sleeping with a woman you love like family."

Penn scowled. "You're making it sound disgusting. Have you never heard of friends with benefits?"

"I've heard of the term but I don't believe in it."

He narrowed his eyes. "Can thousands of millennials who use the phrase be wrong?"

"Honestly, I find it hard to fathom you can sleep with someone you only feel 'friendly' toward." Hayes held up air quotes. "I personally don't sleep with my friends. For me, there has to be a real connection—a spark, the animal magnetism. So, basically, 'friends with benefits' is a big lie."

"Yes, we were obviously far more than friends."

"Tell me something, bro. Do you think about her all the time? Do you miss her? Are you finding it hard to forget her?"

"Well, of course!" Penn threw his hands up. "She's the perfect woman."

Hayes chuckled. "*Flora* is the perfect woman."

"Ha ha, okay. I get it. She's perfect for *me*. I know this. And yes, I can't stop thinking about her. I miss her. Every single day I feel sick about this. But she doesn't want to stay married to me and there isn't a damn thing I can do about it."

"Yes, there is," Hayes came to a stop a few feet from the fence post, turning to face him. "You need to let go of our father's betrayal and move on. And you can if you'll just admit to yourself that you *are* in love with her, whether you want to be or not."

Gia always gave herself a chance to cry. This usually involved an entire day of eating ice cream, staying in her jammies all day, taking long naps, watching sad movies and listening to weepy songs. After that, she declared a moratorium on sadness. No more wallowing. Yes, she loved a man who didn't love her back. *Stop the presses.* She wasn't the first woman to deal with this, and she wouldn't be the last. Their breakup was practical, made sense—and yet, she couldn't stop the tears.

Adele came over as she usually did at least once during these one-day marathons. She brought the soda and popcorn and this time a cake.

"I believe we should eat cake not just to celebrate but to mourn," her bestie said. "Because why is it always just ice cream? Cake belongs, too."

"Any chance to eat cake." Gia lifted the lid. "Why does it say, *'Happy birthday, Petey'*?"

"They were going to throw it out because they misspelled Petey, so they gave it to me cheap. Apparently you spell it Peet,-ie. P-e-e-t, like the coffee company."

"Of course." Gia nodded like this made sense.

She wanted to laugh but she also wanted to cry when she saw the cake had been decorated for a boy who loved airplanes. The cake topper had a runway and two different commercial jetliner planes.

Her thoughts immediately ran to Penn and the memorable night they'd spent together in the middle of a monsoon.

Adele put the soda away in the fridge. "Do you want to watch *Me Before You* or are we talking *Wuthering Heights* level?"

"I gave the ring back." Gia dabbed a tissue on her eyes.

Adele slumped. "*Wuthering Heights* it is, then."

"You don't think I should have given it back," Gia said. "But if I had it now, I'd be wearing it and crying every time I looked at my ring."

"No, I get it, babes. You gotta do what you gotta do." Adele flipped on the gigantic flat-screen and gestured to the couch. "You take a seat and I'll cut a piece of cake."

Obliging, Gia curled up in the fort of pillows she'd made on the sofa earlier today when she took her first nap. She reached for the tissue box. A few minutes later, they were diving into Peetie's airplane cake, a yellow one with a lemon filling and blue buttercream icing.

"Heathcliff," Gia sobbed. "Poor Heathcliff."

"Poor Cathy," Adele muttered and pointed. "What's that?"

She was pointing to the envelope with the wedding night disaster photos. Gia just couldn't bear to put them away. Instead, she kept torturing herself by looking at them over and over again.

"The wedding photos. Today's crying day."

Adele rolled her eyes. She firmly believed in crying for as long as you wanted to and time limits were stupid. However, she also didn't think Marco had even deserved a full *day* of tears.

"Let me take another look-see at these again before you put them away." Adele flipped through the photos, a smile growing with each one until she burst out with a laugh. “These are hilarious! The smiles are a bit too big.”

“Do I need to remind you we’d had too much to drink?”

“Yes, but… I don’t know. Check out how he’s looking at you in this one.” Adele pointed to the photo where Gia was looking directly at the camera when they snapped a photo.

Gia leaned over to see. Penn was not looking at the camera; his eyes were fixed on her.

“He reminds me of…do you remember that guy who won the lottery last year? There were photos of him everywhere—him looking at that check like he couldn’t believe his luck. Like he was the happiest man alive because that check had his name on it. Well, that’s how Penn’s looking at you. *Like he won the lottery.*”

Gia took the photo and studied it. He looked…happy. But whatever he’d felt in that moment, it hadn’t lasted. It didn’t have staying power or she wouldn’t be here watching *Wuthering Heights* and eating her weight in cake.

“I really liked him,” she admitted, plopping her head down in Adele’s lap. “So much.”

“I know, babe.” Adele gently patted her head and listened as loud sobs wracked Gia’s body. “I know.”

Chapter Twenty-Eight

Penn was in such a funk that he had to drag himself back to Hayes's ranch for the get-together Flora had coordinated. He absolutely hated being here again without Gia. It was too soon.

Once again, Flora held a brunch outside in the fresh country air underneath the patio umbrella. Too many memories. This time, however, there were finger sandwiches, various types of salads, chips, beer and iced tea and plenty of Texas barbecue. Oliver showed up, surprising Penn, who made it a point to welcome him. He came alone, like Penn, two bachelors sticking out like extra puzzle pieces that didn't belong to the set.

Penn privately wondered if Oliver had someone in his life, too, someone who made his chest ache like a raw and empty cavity. If so, they'd have even more in common than a cheating father. But hell, he wouldn't wish this agony on his worst enemy. He looked around the table where they had all gathered to eat. Hayes, so deeply in love with Flora it showed in every move he made. Their little boy, Mateo, was the center of their lives and he knew it. The kid would grow up with all the love in the world, never doubting for a second he was wanted. Archibald had failed to give this kind of unconditional love to Hayes, and yet there he was, breaking old patterns with his son.

Madeline, who'd grown up an only child, had found a ready-made family in more than one way. She and her fiancé, Forrest, were helping raise his twin toddler daughters from another marriage. Jillian and Nick Slater, the caretaker of the land Oliver would inherit, were raising his four-year-old niece, and Shelby looked ready to pop a baby. Cameron was quite protective of her, getting up every time she needed something and rubbing her back.

After the lunch, Penn found Oliver standing alone at the edge of the patio.

"It looks like we're the only single men here." Penn handed him a cold beer. "Actually, I'm married, but she's not here. We're going through a rough patch right now."

You can say that again, Penn. Way to understate the problem. Quickie marriage, equally quickie divorce.

"I'm sorry to hear it. At least you loved her enough to marry her. It's hard to believe the kind of relationships my siblings have would ever be possible for me." Oliver accepted the beer. "I'm not exactly keen on love and marriage. I've seen how it destroyed my mother to be ignored and rejected by someone she loved. I never want to be the cause of such pain."

"I used to feel the same way but now I know it's possible to love someone even when you're disillusioned. Even when you've seen the worst in people."

"Yeah?" Oliver seemed genuinely interested.

"I didn't think it would happen to me, either. In fact, I tried hard not to fall in love with her, but I did anyway."

Funny that the first time he confessed being in love with his wife would be to the half brother he didn't even know he had a few months ago. Life was funny sometimes. No, not sometimes. *All the time.*

Oliver nodded. "My mother used to say, 'whatever you resist, persists.' Maybe it's something like that."

"Maybe," Penn said. "All I know is there's no point to keep denying I'm in love with her just because I didn't plan it. It happened and now I have to deal with it."

"Stuff happens," Oliver noted with a shrug. "I mean, look at all this. Who would have thought?"

"Definitely not me. I had one brother my whole life, and now I have two." Penn clapped Oliver on the back.

"Don't forget your sisters," Madeline teased, coming up behind them.

"How could I forget when you're always here to remind me?" Penn quipped back.

"I always wanted a sister," Oliver said.

Jillian joined them. "And you got three!"

"Lucky us." Penn snorted.

Oliver laughed, apparently finding that funny. "You guys are nicer than I thought you'd be. I expected you to be a bunch of stuck-up rich kids I'd never like. But I've given this a lot of thought…and you're right. If I want to understand my family's past, I have to accept the land our father left me."

"Are you sure?" Penn asked. "We don't want to pressure you into doing something before you're ready."

"I am. Thanks for opening up to me, Penn. This hurts, but it's time to face the pain and find out more. Maybe then I can finally have peace." He turned to face everyone, meeting their eyes. "I also want to help you all because you deserve a resolution, too. Our father obviously hurt all of us, but at least we all got to connect once he died. I want to be closer to family. I never had that."

Penn hadn't foreseen that outcome when he unloaded on Oliver about his heartbreak, but maybe voicing a hurt could acknowledge someone else's pain.

"Thank you, Oliver," Madeline said. "I've been waiting for answers for so long."

"We *all* have," Jillian chimed in. "When you're ready, Nick and I will take you to the property."

"How about tomorrow?" Oliver glanced at his watch. "Now that I've made up my mind, I don't want to wait much longer."

Penn could relate with that line of thinking. He didn't want to wait, either. But like any good businessman would, he had to plan. He needed contingencies for how he'd get Gia back. She loved him, and so he had a chance.

"Hey, what's up with you tonight?" Hayes pulled him aside at the end of the evening. "You look like you've lost the deal of the century. Last time you looked this glum you lost the bid on the land you wanted for your resort in Spain."

"Funny you should stay that," Penn said. "I've lost the deal of the century. Gia left me. She doesn't want to stay married."

"Well, brother, what are you going to do about it?"

"Fine, you were right. I love her and I'm going to try like hell to work this out."

That night in his apartment, Penn picked up the annulment papers and read them. The documents would dissolve the marriage of Penn Fortune and Gia Leonetti on the reasons of fraud. He'd read and signed a lot of contracts in his life, but nothing like this one. This would absolve a union like it never happened. But it *had* happened and this dissolution wouldn't change it. The end of this marriage wouldn't take away his memories or the fact she'd always be his first wife, even if not on paper.

Over the past week, memories had come back to him of the night they'd married. Yes, he'd had too much to drink, so his inhibitions were lowered. But he recalled getting married had been *his* idea. They'd gone into his suite and were making out when he'd had the bright idea they should get married.

He still didn't quite know what had come over his logically inclined brain. His thinking skills incapacitated for once, apparently he'd let his heart take the lead.

He remembered suggesting, "Hey, why don't we get married?"

She'd thrown back her head and laughed, obviously thinking he was joking. "Yeah, sure, why don't we?"

"No, I'm *serious*! We have a chapel downstairs."

"Cool," she said. "I've always wanted to see one of those..."

He wasn't sure if she fully realized how serious he was until they were in the gift shop attempting to find a ring that would work. Next thing he knew they were standing in front of the officiant. He recalled being the happiest he'd ever been in his life. Free and light like when he'd been a child, which was the opposite of what he'd expected would come from a marriage.

When the ding from his private elevator came, Penn didn't recognize the woman on the screen. Worried this could be news from the PI, he waited at the elevator doors. The woman looked to be about his age, on the petite side with short dark hair and a shock of pink through it.

"Can I help you?" Penn said when the doors swished closed.

"I hope so. I'm Adele and you don't know me, but I'm your wife's best friend. There's no way she could keep that big a secret from me, and do not judge her for it." Adele twitched her finger.

"I had to tell someone, too."

She nodded. "Right, to get wedding ring advice. By the way, stellar job on the ring. Truly."

"Thanks." Penn lowered his head. He'd done a great job with the jewelry, not so much on the marriage. "Are you here about the annulment papers? Because I haven't had a chance to read them yet. I don't sign anything until I've read it front to back."

"No, I want you to take a look at these." She held out a packet.

Penn recognized the envelope from the Love Chapel at Fortune Resorts. He winced and accepted it. "Our wedding photos. Have you looked at them, too?"

"Yes, and I want you to know they're not nearly as bad as you probably think."

"Oh, I doubt that. But I suppose it's time I take a look."

"Maybe it will bring some memories of that night back or make you realize what you're about to give up?"

"I know exactly what I'm about to lose."

Adele crossed her arms. "I hope that's true. Let me tell you a little about your wife. She's the kindest person I've ever known. When we met as kids, she was my first real friend. My parents struggled but were too proud to accept help, so Gia snuck me clothes she 'outgrew.'" She rolled her eyes and let out a breath. "Which was silly since she's smaller than me—we don't even wear the same size. You know what I mean?" At his puzzled look, she went on. "She was *buying* me clothes, then pretending they no longer fit her. Not sure how she got that past her parents but I went along with it because my mama didn't raise no fool. When we went on field trips and if I didn't have money for a souvenir…or when I was short during the Scholastic Book Fair…well, you get it. She's my best friend for a reason. Your wife is a *saint*."

"None of that surprises me." Penn held up the envelope. "Thank you for these and the walk down memory lane."

The moment the elevator doors closed, he started flipping through them in the hallway outside his apartment. They weren't bad at all. Simply put, he looked happy, similar to the memories he had of that night. They were both standing of their own volition, no one propping them up. He should have known because even after having too much to drink, he'd never do something out of character. He'd married Gia because he *wanted* to, because on some cellular level, he understood she was everything he'd ever wanted. In that altered state of mind, he'd thought he could vault over the conventions of courting someone and go straight to the prize. But those steps were there for a reason.

He had the papers and they wouldn't be valid until *he* signed. Fisting the papers, he ripped them in half, then in fourths. Gia would never accept his former terms, and he was done asking. But maybe he still had a chance if he renegotiated their deal.

There was only one way to find out.

The next day, Penn met with all of his siblings at the property Oliver had inherited. It was on the other side of the railroad tracks, mostly underdeveloped land that for some mysterious reason meant a lot to their father. He'd raised prize horses on the Fortune and Daughters Ranch, but this property had largely been ignored for decades. Empty, the only attractive part of the land was the river that ran through at the southern end.

"Since y'all don't even know what you're looking for, I suggest we all spread out." Nick gestured. "Jillian and I will start on the north end, Madeline and Forrest, take the south, Cameron and Oliver, you take the east, and Hayes and Penn take the west."

"I'm going to let Shelby sit this one out," Cameron said, pointing to his pregnant wife.

Today the Texas heat sweltered down in waves, the humidity punishing. Hats could only do so much in the pursuit of shade. A drop of sweat rolled down Penn's back. It would be nice if someone turned the sun down a notch. Nick had brought shovels and axes and tools for poking around in the dirt but it seemed hopeless to Penn. If anything was buried out here, they'd have to comb every inch of ground to find it. Some clues would be good. Clues on a map, even better. There was a reason *X* marked the spot. But, he supposed, they could come out here every weekend and dig.

"If I were our dad," Penn said to Hayes, shoveling in a pile of dirt a few feet away. "Where would I hide something I didn't want anyone else to find?"

"Exactly," Hayes muttered. "This could take forever if we don't have the first idea of where to look."

"I don't know about you, but I hate wasting my time," Penn said, hitting something hard, only to bend down and discover a rock almost the size of a boulder.

Two hours later, zero progress had been made and there were several piles of dirt from one end of the property to the other.

"This is impossible!" Jillian burst out, throwing down her shovel.

"Well, how badly do you want to find this?" Nick said, picking it up.

Jillian sighed. "Pretty badly."

"We all do," Hayes said.

"Hey, how about we all move down to the river side? It will at least give us a relief from this heat," Madeline suggested.

No one complained or argued any further, Penn leading the way forward. If this humidity got much worse, he'd be jumping into that river—clothes and all—for a quick, swim. *That* would be refreshing.

"Hey, isn't this where Archibald wanted his ashes scattered?" Madeline pointed to a little bend in the river, where a large willow tree's branches bent, as if reaching into the water. “By the river, near the tree with branches that dip into the stream.”

“I remember that,” Penn said. “It’s a clue, at least.”

Once they called everyone over to the area, they all began to dig. Focusing in one area made this go a lot faster. Still, it was another hour before Penn hit something hard with his shovel, and this time it wasn’t a rock.

He dug around it with his hands. “Found something.”

“What is it?” Hayes leaned over. “It looks like a metallic toy.”

“Yeah, probably something no one intended to bury.” But as Penn and Hayes both worked around the metal, they found a box. Definitely *not* a toy.

Madeline walked over to examine it. “It’s a tin box.”

The box had a lid but was essentially something relegated from its original purpose. Decorated with bright colors, it had apparently once carried envelopes of hot chocolate mix inside. Everyone surrounded him as Penn placed it on the ground. Oliver was the first to lean down and pry open the lid. It felt like they’d all waited on him to do it.

Penn watched as his brother removed what looked like a small, old and faded three-ring notebook.

“It’s a journal,” Oliver whispered, flipping the page. “And there are old pictures. Look, that’s my mother in this photo.”

Penn leaned closer to better see, and before long they were all hanging over Oliver’s shoulder. There were photos of Hayes and Penn when they were little. Photos of their mother, too.

“That’s me and Taffy,” Madeline said, pointing. “I was about five. We went to get a professional family photo taken but…he didn’t show up.”

Oliver handed her the photo, and soon Jillian had the pictures of her and Shelby, along with their mother. Penn and Hayes took their photos, too.

Sadly, here were no photos of baby Oliver because Archibald had never been in touch after Lianna got pregnant. She must have left soon after telling Archibald about the baby and changed her name. A spark of fury flared at the thought that Penn's father had turned away his pregnant mistress, leaving her to fend for herself. He couldn't imagine what Oliver was feeling, but with any luck, he was more forgiving than Penn.

"I never knew him," Oliver said, his voice husky. "This is the closest I'll ever come. An old journal which belonged to him, photos, and a piece of land."

For one long moment, no one said a word.

Hayes broke the silence. "The journal might explain his history and why he did the things he did."

Madeline took the journal and flipped through the pages. "There's a lot in here. His thoughts, his plans. And look—he started writing about the time he would have been eighteen."

That would coincide with when he became an orphan and the turn of events that led him to eventually become a billionaire. It would make for interesting reading.

"We should all read this," Oliver said. "So we can understand him better."

"We at least had bits and pieces of our father over the years." Madeline touched Oliver's shoulder. "You never had the chance to know him. You should read the journal first."

"I agree," said Penn.

"I second that." Hayes nodded.

In short order, everyone else agreed Oliver should take the journal home with him.

"I'll let y'all know when I'm done with it," Oliver said. "And then everyone can read it."

Chapter Twenty-Nine

Penn helped Nick put away all the shovels and pickaxes they'd used to dig up several holes all over the land. Hayes was filling in some of the holes with Cameron's help.

"We left you a mess." Penn shook his head. "Thank goodness the old man wanted to have his ashes scattered by that tree."

Nick chuckled. "For a good cause. I'm glad Jillian will have answers soon."

"Hey, don't forget Kate Fortune's hundredth birthday party in a few weeks," Madeline called out. "You'll all be there, right?"

Right. Penn did *not* want to be there. Not if he couldn't have Gia with him.

It might have been his expression that made Madeline keep talking. "There will be Fortunes from all across Texas there, like Jerome Fortune. The royal Fortunes too, and they're even going to have the Cowboy Country USA amusement park mini replica I've been creating"

"Sounds…interesting." But Oliver sounded as interested as Penn felt.

"The kids will *love* the amusement park." Madeline had started to sound like a used car salesman.

"Yeah, I don't have kids," Penn said.

"Same," Oliver echoed.

"You can come help me with Mateo." Hayes hooked an arm around Penn, obviously not allowing him to weasel out of this. "He loves his Uncle Penn."

"That's a low blow," Penn muttered. "You know how I adore that kid."

"It starts at five," Jillian said.

"You have no excuse now," Hayes said with a smile. "Just take the elevator downstairs."

"They have that huge private ballroom and Kate says we'll stay until she says it's over," Shelby said, hand on her belly. "But I'll probably be in bed by nine."

"How exactly is our father connected to Kate Fortune, anyway?" Penn assumed he would have heard of an aunt or grandmother, so she couldn't be immediate family.

"I still don't know." Madeline shrugged. "There's no known history between them, at least not that anyone's uncovered. Kate told me it was our father who recommended me for the job of planning the party. But she's thirty years older than Archibald and they weren't from the same part of Texas."

"But clearly," Hayes said, "they knew each other *somehow*."

"Maybe he wrote about her in the journal," Oliver said. "If he did, we'll soon have some answers."

"Did you get any more word from that reclusive actress? What's her name again?" Hayes scratched his temple.

"Susannah Simmons," Madeline said. "I'm hoping she'll mysteriously show up at the party. She's Kate's estranged great-great-grandniece, and some folks on social media are wondering if the reason she disappeared from the spotlight is because she was disfigured in a car accident. But no one knows, it's just a rumor."

Penn didn't miss the way Oliver physically recoiled at the

mention of Susannah's name. Did he know her, or was he especially sensitive to the idea of a terrible accident?

Later, as Penn was getting in his car to leave, Madeline approached him. "Did you see Oliver's expression when I mentioned Susannah?"

"Yeah," Penn said. "What was that about? Does he know her?"

"I doubt it. Maybe he's just a true fan who's concerned and wondering what's going on with her." She elbowed Penn. "Oh, hey, I meant to ask. Did she like the ring?"

"It was a big hit."

"Great! Happy to help. Is this whole thing going to be a secret much longer? Because I'm terrible with secrets." She lowered her head. "I told Forrest. I'm sorry. But unlike me, he's really good at keeping secrets."

Penn smirked. "It's all right. Soon, *everyone* is going to know."

"How could she say no to that ring?"

Penn nodded because she'd said yes the first time. She might do it again. "I'm lucky."

"That sounds exciting! Another big wedding, I hope?"

"You and me both." Then Penn got in his sedan and drove off, because he had a lot of planning to do.

Nothing cured Gia's doldrums like a day at the vineyard. Maybe her family were all a bit worried about her, because Mama and her sisters had called and asked her to come by this afternoon. The timing was perfect, the summer skies clear and bright. Today, she'd talk to Papa Enzo and Mama about moving back. Picturing life here with Penn had confirmed her decision. She'd made a mistake with her luxury condo and hated living in what felt like a monument to technology. She appreciated tech as much as the next person but a "smart" house was too much. The other day, the app had announced her favorite toothpaste was on sale, and would she like to place it in the cart.

Startled, Gia, had shouted, "No, thank you!"

She couldn't live like this, talking to machines. An old-fashioned girl at heart, she wanted low-tech houses where she had to pull back the window shades using the magic of her own hands. She yearned to be closer to family, and the man she'd one day marry would have to accept this was how she wanted to live. This was her past and would also be her future.

She found Mama and her sisters in the kitchen making homemade pasta, straining it through the machine. Not all people understood how much better it tasted when it was homemade and not store-bought. Gia breezed in and kissed her mother's cheek, then hugged Bella and Antonia. Tonight, she'd tell them what had happened with Penn.

"What are you making for dinner?" Gia asked, looking forward to her mother's cooking.

"It's for tomorrow," Mama said. "The sauce is already made. We might have a celebration."

"Oh? What's the occasion?"

Her sisters and mother all exchanged conspiratorial smiles. This couldn't be good.

"Don't tell me you're trying to fix me up again!" Gia threw her hands up. "No! Fermati! I'll find my own dates and I'm not going to be dating anyone for a while. My heart needs time to heal."

"So, you're decided?" Antonia fisted hands on hips. "You're going through with the annulment?"

"I don't think I have a choice." Gia lowered her head. "I took your advice and brought the papers to Penn. I asked him to tear them up if he wanted to have a real marriage. He didn't. So, that's the end."

"That must be why you didn't answer my texts yesterday," Bella said softly. "You were in the middle of your crying day."

Gia nodded. "I knew you'd understand."

"Well, now that you're here I need your advice," her older sister said.

"No, I don't think you should call the wine Amore. That's too cliché." Gia shook her head. "I'll think of a better marketing campaign. Just give me a few days."

"That's not what I meant. I wanted your advice, out in the vineyard." Bella pointed.

"In the *vineyard*? How can I be of any help? I know nothing about grapes."

"You know a lot more than you realize. And I think it's time I taught you some basics."

"Really?" Gia brightened because Bella was territorial about the vines, and the entire process.

It seemed her sister had finally judged Gia worthy of the secrets of winemaking. Not that she didn't know some of them already, but the thought Bella wanted to teach her the ways of Leonetti wine making thrilled Gia to the core.

"Actually, I've always said I could better sell the wine if you'd let me see all the facets."

"I know, and I finally want to show you."

Gia followed Bella down the front porch steps, and they walked casually in tune toward the vines. As always, memories flooded back—how she'd once set up a blanket between two rows to make a fort. Later, after scolding her, Papa Enzo had agreed that being outside, with the sweet scent of grapes wafting in the air, was the best thing in the world.

"Where are we going?" Not exactly having worn walking shoes, Gia rushed to keep up with Bella.

They climbed the small hill, Bella always leading the way. Until she took off at a run.

"Bella! I'm wearing heels. Slow *down*!" Gia bent to adjust her sandal strap and catch her breath.

Then she heard a voice calling to her, one that sounded achingly familiar.

"Gia." Penn stepped out from a row two ahead of her.

He wore jeans and boots with a green pearl-button short-sleeve shirt that matched his eyes.

"What are *you* doing here?" She still hadn't caught her breath, not just from sprinting to catch Bella but simply from the sight of him.

"Something I should have done a while ago." He held out his hand, which she accepted, and he led her into the row labeled Cabernet Sauvignon.

What she saw before her was a fairy-tale scene. In between the two rows stood a table with two chairs, but Gia's heart skipped a beat at the canopy above them, decorated with blinking fairy lights. Flowers hung from one end to the other. Her childhood fantasy in adult format. A vase with colorful orange and yellow daylilies sat as the centerpiece. She took it all in, wondering when and how Penn had managed to pull all this off. It was clear her family had been in on it.

"Yes, I had help from your family," Penn said, reading her mind. "I told your mother and sisters that I was in love with you but like an idiot, I'd screwed it all up. They agreed, of course—I *was* an idiot—but lucky for me offered to help me fix it."

Gia brought a hand up to her racing heart. "You're finally admitting you love me?"

She hadn't been wrong. She hadn't been fooled by her own desires. This *was* real.

"Yes." He took her two hands in his and brought them to his lips. "There was a reason I didn't want to end this marriage and it wasn't convenience. Yes, we're good together, but it's a lot more than that. Ever since we broke up, I can't eat. I can't sleep without you next to me. Clearly, I'm in love. You're my whole heart, Gia, and I adore you."

Gia's eyes teared up because he was saying all the right things again and she wanted more than anything to believe him. But *could* she? When and how had he changed his mind?

"I think I knew it from the moment I saw you in my office. Love at first sight. I didn't think that was a real thing, so I talked myself out of it. But then… I saw the wedding photos. It's clear to me that you were what I wanted that night, drunk or not, and you're what I want every night for the rest of my life. I'm talking about forever. You called me your first, but I also want to be the last. *I'm* going to be your only husband."

"But what about the—" she began.

"I tore up the annulment papers."

"You did?" Her heart cracked open.

"In half and then in fourths. They were confetti when I was done with them. You know I never wanted an annulment because we could never erase what happened between us. It was *real.* But now I realize the first time this happened I didn't actually ask you to marry me. I believe I suggested it and you agreed."

He paused, his voice breaking with emotion. He pressed his forehead gently to hers, closing his eyes for a moment before continuing.

"Staying married has to be more than something convenient or making the best out of an arrangement because we fell into it. I always wanted this and I still do. I'm in love with you, Gia, and I look forward to falling more in love with you every day, every week, every month, every year. *Every decade.* I want to live here on the farm with you. And I want *our* children to run though these fields the way you did and grow up knowing they have parents who love each other."

"Oh, Penn—"

"Hang on." He dropped to one knee. "I need to do this the right way this time. You're a traditional lady and I love that about you. I already asked your mother and grandfather, which is why I'm here. They approve. Now I'm officially asking you, even if you're already technically my wife. Will you marry me again, please?"

"Yes, however many times you want. Thank you for asking. Yes, yes, yes!" She pulled Penn up and kissed him hard, wrapping her arms around him, putting her entire body into the kiss.

He slipped the ring back on her hand with ease. "And don't take that off again. Please."

"I never will."

He kissed her again, drawing her to him, and she felt his strong heartbeat against her chest. When they broke for air, Bella stood at the end of the row, holding a bottle of wine she'd uncorked and shouting for the rest of the family to join them.

"Let's make a toast with the wine which helped get you into this wonderful situation in the first place. And I'm calling it Amore, you can't stop me!"

Gia didn't want to stop her anymore, even if it was cliché, tired or overused, because she had a gooey center filled with the kind of happiness you couldn't squeeze out of a grape.

"We're getting married twice," Penn announced. "So it will stick."

Antonia, Mama, Papa Enzo and the children circled them.

"Congratulazioni," Papa Enzo said. "Alla famiglia!"

"To our family," Penn said, brushing a kiss on her neck.

They raised a glass to family, to the ones they had, and the one they'd soon create.

Epilogue

Two weeks later, on the night of Penn and Gia's last-minute, post-engagement party, there were questions. So many questions.

"What do you mean you're *already* married?" Jillian said. "I'm so confused."

"You said you were going to ask her to marry you and I heard she accepted a couple of weeks ago," Madeline blurted. "So, how's this a *post*-engagement party?"

"Did you elope?" Jillian asked.

"In a manner of speaking." Penn cleared his throat. "Believe me, I hated keeping any of this a secret. I wanted to shout it from the rooftops, but I had to respect my bride's wishes. Just think of this as a small reception prior to the main one. I know, it's confusing."

He and Gia wanted to celebrate their first Las Vegas marriage with everyone, but they couldn't very well have an engagement party when they were already married. A wedding reception wasn't appropriate yet, either, as early next year they'd be married in the church to appease Gia's mother. Afterwards, they'd have the official wedding reception. At least, that was his understanding. There were plenty of moving parts and Gia and her sisters were taking care of most of the details.

Penn grabbed a couple of flutes from the passing tray and

handed them out to his sisters. "I would have asked for your help in planning this but you're busy enough with the hundredth birthday celebration."

"Yes, that's true," Madeline said. "But I will be putting in a bid for the official wedding reception."

They'd decided to hold the engagement party at Leonetti Vineyards, site of his official proposal, and a perfect setting. The lush green lawn at the bottom of the hill of crops had been decorated with flowers and white lights, and covered by a large white canopy.

"Where's the honeymoon going to be?" Shelby asked.

"Wherever she wants," Penn said. "But we've been talking about the Italian countryside…"

Oliver joined them, holding his own flute of champagne and chuckling. "Can't believe you actually got married in Vegas."

"It was the best thing I ever *did* there." Penn cleared his throat. "Have you finished reading the journal yet?"

Oliver nodded. "What I read made me feel closer to him, and to all of you. It was…a lot to digest, but let's just say I'm glad I know. It's brought me peace."

"Good for you," said Penn.

He hoped it would do the same for him. For all of them.

"And I've decided to change my name to Oliver Fortune Dunhill to honor both of my parents." Oliver handed the journal to Shelby. "You and Jillian should read it next."

Shelby clutched the journal to her bosom. "I need some juicy reading material."

"Well, I didn't say it was *juicy*," Oliver interjected.

"It kind of goes without saying. I get it next," Jillian said.

"Sounds like we're going in birth order," Penn smirked. "Hayes and I are next. But I'm going to be busy moving to the Leonetti quarters."

"In that case, I'll pass it on to Madeline when I'm done," Hayes said.

Sooner or later, maybe they'd all come to an understanding of Archibald and why he'd made some of the decisions he had. It might help bring everyone some closure. As for Penn, he'd gained a new insight into himself through the process of his whirlwind marriage to Gia. Sometimes the best things in life were unplanned and if you had the courage to stick it through, some truly wonderful things could emerge.

He met wife's gaze from across the room where she was speaking with some of their guests. Dressed in a short gold dress and matching heels, her dark hair up, she looked positively edible to him. She smiled back, the wicked "*I see you*" smile that did all manner of things to him. He'd been angry when hearing she'd had annulment papers in her purse but it was her sister Antonia who explained to Penn that Gia had simply been trying to make things easier for him. Which sounded very much like her.

"Time for cake!"

Madeline drew them all out to the center of the canopy where there was a small, tiered cake waiting for them decorated in yellow—Gia's favorite color—and white. His only requirement was that the cake should have plenty of raspberry filling…and no saffron.

That had made Gia laugh. The whole saffron incident had become a private joke between them. Whenever they'd talk about dinner plans he'd shout, "Please, God, anything but saffron!"

"I'd like to make a toast to my beautiful bride," Penn said, raising his flute. "When I first came to Emerald Ridge, I have to admit I didn't do it happily. I was angry and bitter about many things. Then I met this wonderful woman and everything changed. I'm lucky she gave me a chance. I love you, Gia Leonetti."

"Woo-hoo!" came the shouts from their family and friends.

"See? That isn't so hard, is it?" Hayes called out, making everyone laugh.

"I loved you first," Gia said, going into his arms.

They could debate that all night, but he would let her have it.

"But I love you more."

* * * * *